Do you have a Matchmaking Mother from Hell? Take our test and find out... if you dare.

Your mother thinks you should attract a man by:

a) Being your charming, witty self.

b) Offering to make him a home-cooked meal.

c) Stealing his child.

Your mother thinks the perfect man for you would be:

a) Tom Cruise.

b) A nineties version of Robert Young in "Father Knows Best."

c) Your cousin's fiancé.

Your mother thinks family planning is:

a) Birth control.

b) Inviting the whole family to a huge Fourth of July picnic.

c) Having her run your life until the day you die.

If you chose A most often: Ever thought of hiring your mother out? You'd make a mint. She sounds like a dream come true.

If you chose B most often: Look at the bright side—you'll never get out of the kitchen long enough to find out if you even like the guy!

If you chose C most often: You truly have a matchmaking mother from hell. Beware, but just in case, be sure to keep candy on hand for the kids she swipes from gorgeous divorcés.

Dear Reader,

Several months ago we editors took a group of LOVE & LAUGHTER authors to dinner. While each and every one of these smart, funny ladies can talk and talk and talk, each and every one of us at the table had to give in to new Harlequin author Cheryl Anne Porter. She is a woman who is met with the line "Why don't you do stand-up?" over and over again. By the end of the dinner, all we could do was sit with tears rolling down our cheeks, clutching our sides with laughter as Cheryl entertained with yet another rollicking anecdote. Cheryl also writes historical romances, but *A Man in Demand* is her first contemporary and another great addition to the Matchmaking Moms From Hell miniseries.

Not to be outdone is Lisa Bingham, a relative newcomer to the Harlequin family but a huge sensation. Her Harlequin American Romance stories, including *Nanny Jake* and *The Daddy Hunt,* have been incredibly popular with readers. We're very pleased to include her in the LOVE & LAUGHTER lineup with *Runner-Up Bride.*

Next month brings a wonderful surprise: Let's Celebrate, a special promotion running for three months. And there's a really cool contest for you to enter. Look for all the details next month. Wishing you much love and laughter,

Malle Vallik

Malle Vallik
Associate Senior Editor

A MAN IN DEMAND
Cheryl Anne Porter

Harlequin Books

TORONTO • NEW YORK • LONDON
AMSTERDAM • PARIS • SYDNEY • HAMBURG
STOCKHOLM • ATHENS • TOKYO • MILAN
MADRID • WARSAW • BUDAPEST • AUCKLAND

ISBN 0-373-44021-9

A MAN IN DEMAND

Copyright © 1997 by Cheryl Anne Porter

This edition published by arrangement with Harlequin Books S.A.

® and TM are trademarks of the publisher. Trademarks indicated with ® are registered in the United States Patent and Trademark Office, the Canadian Trade Marks Office and in other countries.

Printed in U.S.A.

A funny thing happened...

I won't come right out and say I have a Matchmaking Mama. But it's an unspoken rule in our family that we marry the mate Mom picks for us. The penalty for noncompliance is Mom keeping our Intended and giving us the boot. Lucky for me and my brother Jimmie, we fell in love with our Chosen Ones. But Mom has to keep busy, so now she's working on my sister Paula and brother Mark.

—Cheryl Anne Porter

A MAN IN DEMAND is Cheryl Anne Porter's debut into the contemporary market. And what an entrance she's made! Be sure to watch for upcoming madcap stories by this talented author.

To my husband, Paul, whom I love dearly.
And it's a good thing because you were also
Mom's choice for me.

To my editor, Brenda Chin, who absolutely
refuses to allow me to say "Bless your heart" in any
connotation with her. Brenda, you're the best.

To my closest friend, Christy Ruth
(first and last name, not just her Southern name).
You're in my heart, girl.

To Mom, who always— What? I *am* sitting up straight.
No, I haven't put on weight. My hair?
What's wrong with my hair? Hey, Mom, look—
Paula and Mark aren't married yet!

1

"OHMIGOD, MOTHER, what have you done now?" Julie kicked her own mental behind for not suspecting, before she even opened her apartment door, that Mayhem, and not Opportunity, was in the breezeway and knocking.

For, sure enough, framed in the open doorway stood Mayhem. In all her radiant, red-haired, grandmotherly glory. In one arm, she balanced a brimming grocery bag and her huge orange purse. Holding her other hand was a dark-haired little boy who couldn't be more than three years old.

"Mother, where did you get this child? You are not coming in until you take him back." Julie pointed the way toward the parking lot. "Now."

Her mother ignored her gesture in favor of beaming at her and then down at the boy, whose jaws worked furiously around a sucker. Then her gaze moved back to her daughter, and she crowed, "This would be perfect if it were Valentine's Day! Because this time, I've found the right man. Meet your future husband!"

Julie looked from her mother to the little boy, and back again. "Don't you think he's kind of young?"

Her mother made a dismissive sound. "Not him. Him!"

She released the boy's hand, shifted the bag to her other arm and reached out, only to drag into Julie's view…the Hunk. In Levi's and a red-and-white Oklahoma Sooners T-shirt. Shock brought Julie's hands to her face.

The Hunk? Mother brought her the Hunk? Every woman in the apartment complex was in love with him. The com-

*plex? Heck, in all of Brandon. Maybe in all of Florida.
Julie's insides shriveled when she took a mental inventory
of herself. Barefoot, cutoff shorts and a raggedy T-shirt.
And no makeup. Or bra.*

"Hi. Happy a-week-early Valentine's Day."

Julie knew she was staring, but she couldn't stop herself.
The man was gorgeous.

"Say something to him, honey. It's no wonder you're
pushing thirty and still single."

Julie felt the natural curl in her hair straighten out. She
moved her hands about two inches away from her mouth.
Oh, she'd say something, all right. "Mother, how could
you?"

"Tell him your age? Well, he'd have to know before
you go for your marriage license."

"Mother!" Julie astounded herself by actually shrieking.
She took a deep, calming breath. And started over. "Not
that—well yes, that, too. But I mean, how could you—"
Words suddenly failed her, so she settled for gesturing at
the Hunk and his son. "Them, Mother. How could you?"

"Oh, that wasn't hard at all. I caught them in the parking
lot when I drove in. Here, take these groceries I brought
you. You wouldn't eat if I didn't bring you food."

Automatically taking the offered paper bag, Julie only
dimly heard the last of her mother's familiar harangue.
She'd stopped listening at the words "caught them." There
was no huge net in her mother's hands. So, maybe she was
speaking figuratively. But with Ida Cochran, you took nothing for granted. "You…caught them how?"

"Maybe I can shed some light here?"

Julie transferred her attention to the captured man. "I'm
not sure God could shed light where my mother is concerned, but please try." She set the bag down inside her
apartment and then straightened up, hands to her waist,
ready to listen.

But he wasn't talking. The Hunk was, instead, openly
staring at her. Pinned by the intensity of his gaze, Julie

returned the compliment. *Oh, boy. He was one of those men who just got better up close.*

Mercifully, he stared at her for only a moment longer before he gave a slight shake of his head, and then bent over to set down his own bags. Not so mercifully, he managed to do so in one fluid movement of toned and rippling muscles that momentarily stole Julie's breath.

Straightening up, he launched into his version. "Mrs. Cochran here caught us—to use her word—as we were unloading our groceries down in front of our apartment. She introduced herself and then asked me if I'd met her daughter. When I said no, she insisted that I needed to. And—" he gestured between himself and his son "—here we are." He glanced down at his son again and did a double take. "Where'd you get that candy, Aaron?"

The boy popped the sucker out of his mouth. "From this grandma-lady. Can I have it?"

"Well, yeah, since it's about half gone, I guess you can." He turned to Julie's mother. "You couldn't ask?"

Her embarrassment at her mother's behavior finally won over Julie's fascination with watching the Hunk speak. Julie confronted her mother. "You gave this child candy without asking his father?"

"I asked him, and he nodded yes." She waved her hand dismissively and smiled. "But it doesn't matter. We'll work on teaching Aaron not to take candy from strangers. I don't want to have to worry about my step-grandson being snatched by some loony."

"As if it hasn't just happened, Mother."

But her mother dismissed her with another wave of her hand and began sorting through her orange purse.

Giving up, Julie turned again to the Hunk. Seeing the poor guy's quizzical look, she bit back a chuckle. Ten bucks said he was sifting through the events that had led him to her apartment door. He'd probably nodded fifty times on the way over. That's all most people could do because Ida didn't converse. She "monologued." Still, half of Julie expected the tanned specimen of all-that-was-right-with-men to reach for her mother's throat. Or hoped he would.

But he just looked befuddled. "Maybe I did say it was okay. I can't remember."

When his frown intensified, Julie stepped in. "Mother, do you realize that you've taken advantage here? You have been completely out of control for the past month with this husband thing. I swear, you're just lucky that he—excuse me, what's your name?"

"Mike."

"Mike here didn't call the authorities."

"No need," Mike said. "I am the authorities."

Julie's gaze froze on him. *Oh, Lordy.* She turned to her mother. "He's a policeman?"

He put up a hand to capture her attention. "Worse. FBI."

"FBI?" she squeaked.

"Yep. And I have to ask you, does she do this a lot?"

They both looked at her mother. Ida was bent over the little boy and wiping his hands with a tissue.

Despite everything, a rush of loving tolerance for her mother coursed through Julie. She shrugged at the Hunk and gave him a lopsided grin. "She just thinks I ought to be married and not so obsessed—her word—with my career. So she brings home anyone she thinks is good husband material." Julie rolled her eyes. "I am so embarrassed right now I could happily dry up and blow away."

He grinned. "No harm done." Then his expression sobered. "You're a 'career first' woman, huh? I've had some experience with that. It can make life…interesting. But it's none of my business." Then he grinned again. "Yeah, it is. I am the husband-candidate du jour, right?"

"Right. Sorry." She shrugged her shoulders, totally undone by his smiling good humor in the face of such a bizarre situation. And she couldn't help being a little curious about his experience with a "career-first woman." What did that mean? Still, with nothing left to say, she could only return his dark, intense gaze that was sizzling her skin.

Suddenly, her mother straightened up, capturing their attention. It was a good thing, too, because Julie knew she and the Hunk were in serious danger of again staring too long at each other.

"Well, I don't know," Ida fussed. "You looked so perfect, Mike. But an FBI agent? You weren't joking, were you?"

Mike raised an eyebrow. "No, ma'am. There are laws against impersonating a federal officer."

"I was afraid of that." Sighing, she turned to her daughter. "Will you worry at night when he's out on the streets?"

Mike raised his other eyebrow. Julie jumped in. "She watches too much TV."

He nodded his head in understanding. Or sympathy. "We're not all out on the…streets. Not like you're thinking, ma'am."

No. Don't encourage her. Run. Save yourself and your child. Tell her you have a wife. Tell her you have a wife and a horrible, communicable disease—which is hereditary. Mike needed to know it wasn't safe for him to have a polite, revealing conversation with her mother. Not when Ida was on a sacred quest to find a mate for her youngest child, the only one not yet married of Jack and Ida Cochran's three kids.

"So-o-o, you're not on the streets?" Too late. Ida smiled, the sly one that Julie knew sent her father scurrying to the golf course. Ida opened her purse and pulled out a legal pad and a pencil.

Oh, no. Not The Questionnaire for Prospective Husbands! Julie held up her hands in a don't-you-even-dare gesture. "No, Mother. The nice man has a son. Therefore, he probably also has a wife." *Please don't let him have a wife. Please don't—*

"No, I don't." The big, beautiful, dumb man had just cut his own throat.

He doesn't have a wife. He doesn't have a wife. Julie's mental celebration was cut short when she saw her mother check something off her list. "I was right. No wedding ring."

"You should never have admitted that." Julie turned a pitying expression on Mike, whose gaze darted from her to Ida.

"Now," Ida proclaimed, erasing something from her notepad. "Why don't you have a wife?"

A deadly silence ensued. Julie noticed that, despite the time of year, it was definitely getting warm around here. She jumped into action. "That does it." Before the nice FBI agent could explode and kill her mother, Julie snatched Ida into her apartment and yelled "Run!" to the two males outside. Then she closed the door in their faces. Turning to her mother, she put her hands on her hips.

Ida gestured frantically toward the closed door. "Julie! He'll get away. He's perfect, honey—"

Julie held up her hand to stop the tirade she knew was coming. She then cocked an ear toward the door, listening to the faint, crackling sounds of paper bags being lifted. "Just a minute. They're not gone yet."

Her mother huffed, picked up the bag of groceries she'd brought and turned to walk into the kitchen. "Oh, fine, then I'll just put these away. Do you have any chocolate?"

"Go see, Mom." Waiting until her mother rounded the corner, Julie gave in to her hunch that told her to check outside. She opened the door. Yep. Again holding their grocery bags, the sacrificial ram and his little lamb were still standing there. "If you value your freedom, Mike, you will pack up your belongings and your son and run as far as you can."

He chuckled. "You know what? This is funny." Then, giving her a sidelong glance, he sobered. "I've been standing here thinking—why *are* you unattached? I mean, someone who looks like you. So, Julie, is there something you need to tell your mother? Such as, you don't like men?''

Julie's eyes widened. "Of course I like men! I love men! Lots of them! No, not lots. I mean, I just haven't— My job just—'' She gave up protesting when she saw his teasing grin. Crossing her arms, she glared at him. "Whose side are you on, anyway?''

His grin changed to the most seductive, leering smile she'd ever seen. "The men's, but we'll never win the war of the sexes. We like fraternizing with the enemy too much.''

Julie sputtered in protest, sounding embarrassingly similar to her BMW when it slipped a gear. While Mike displayed that secret man's grin, meant to confound women, she had to settle for glaring until she could mentally shift out of Park.

Just then, a child's voice broke the stalemate. "Where's your grandma-lady?''

She looked down at…Aaron, wasn't it? He was a beautiful black-haired, black-eyed replica of his drop-dead gorgeous father. She'd forgotten he was there—that's how rattled she was. "My grandma-lady had to go away. She's been very, very bad—like some other people I know,'' she said, staring pointedly at the boy's father.

"Oh.'' Aaron recaptured her attention and frowned, wiping his hands, still red and grimy from the remains of his sucker, on his white T-shirt.

Julie winced. There went the laundry.

"What did her do that was bad?''

How was she to answer that? She looked from Aaron to his father. And caught Mike checking her out. Again. The look in his eyes made Julie's blood rush through her veins at a crazy pace and made her forget he'd been baiting her.

In a husky voice, he echoed his son's question. "Yeah, what did she do that was so bad?''

Think, Julie. And don't stare. "Well, she brought you

here, pretty much against your will, and she gave Aaron candy—"

"It will be Valentine's Day soon."

Julie experienced a moment of terror when she realized that the longer she stood there staring, the less capable she was of completing a thought, much less a sentence. What had they been talking about?

A movement from Aaron finally brought her out of her daze, and she looked down at him again. With a childish lack of aplomb, he'd set about digging at the seat of his shorts. "I can't have candy from stranglers. But your grandma's not one of them, huh?"

Stranglers. Her grandmother. Hah. "Well, sweetie, from here—" she peeked behind the door to see her mother nibbling at a bag of chocolate chips while she read the recipes on the back "—I'd say she's pretty strange."

Ida looked up. "Julie, I swear. The freshness date on these chips has come and gone. How do you expect to keep a child alive if you can't even keep chocolate chips from expiring?"

Julie shook her head and looked back at Mike, as if to say, "Now do you understand?"

"You have my utmost sympathy."

"Thank you, Mike." She laughed at his formal tone. "I don't think I can hold her much longer. You'd better go."

"I think you're right. The cold, wet stuff I'm feeling on my arm is probably melted ice cream. Well, if you ever need the FBI, call me. And somehow, I think you will."

Will what? Need the FBI? Or call him? Julie suspected she was melting at a faster pace than the ice cream she so desperately wanted to lick off his skin. *Okay, where was this lusting stuff coming from? Maybe her mother was right. Maybe she was spending too much time number-crunching at the bank. Maybe she did need to get out more.*

As the moment stretched out, Julie became aware that she and Mike were still staring at each other. Just as her last shred of female decency threatened to tear and send her leaping into the man's arms, Mike saved her by clearing his throat and dragging his gaze away to speak to his son. "Come on, hotshot. Let's go put this stuff away, and then we'll go for a workout in the gym. Are you game?"

When his son nodded enthusiastically, Mike turned his assessing gaze on Julie, looking her up and down. "See you around."

She should have been offended at his blatant mental undressing of her, but she was too busy trying to picture him in a sweaty T-shirt and tight shorts. When he cocked his head at her, Julie realized that he was expecting an answer. "What?"

"I said I'd see you around, as in a parting comment."

She nodded and grinned, probably stupidly. How was it possible for one man to be such a walking poster boy for sexuality? *Whoa. The man is a father. He has his child with him. Say something—something decent, preferably.* "Um, sure. See you around. I'm just going to go kill my mother."

He gaped at her for a moment and then laughed. "Okay, but when the cops come, I know nothing. Fair enough?"

"Sure. All's fair in love and war, as they say."

When his expression changed to let her know she'd just grown braying-jackass ears, Julie struggled, by sheer will, to douse the hot flush that claimed her cheeks. *Oh, God.*

"Uh, yeah. Love and war. Well, I have to go. Come on, Aaron." Shaking his head, he turned away.

For the next few moments, Julie stared after the Hunk's departing derriere. With a heavy sigh, she stepped back inside and closed the door. As soon as she did, mortified reaction set in. She needed to scream. Hoping to muffle it from her neighbors, she leaped for her flower-patterned couch and plunged face-first onto the overstuffed cushions, burrowing her face into them. And then she screamed.

Coming up for air, she braced herself on her elbows. Her mother, one hip perched over the back of the couch, calmly reached out and smoothed the hair out of Julie's face, completely unaware, apparently, that her baby was engaging in primal screaming—on her account.

"Your hair's getting long, honey. You really need to go in for a cut. I swear, your hair's as red as mine. I always wanted you kids to have your father's coloring."

Julie stared at her mother as if she'd never seen her before. "Well, at least Susan and Dan have Dad's blond, blue-eyed coloring. Two out of three ain't bad."

"Don't say 'ain't.' Men will think you're not educated. But I suppose there's nothing wrong with your red hair. I hear it's all the rage now. Still, if only you had green eyes to go with it, instead of your grandmother's icy blue ones. Hey, why don't you get some colored contacts?"

Julie looked at the cushions under her. *Get ready for another round,* she warned them. Then, turning on her side, she cupped her cheek in her hand and looked at her mother. *What a riot she was. And an absolute bulldog when it came to her children. She'd see them happy, even if it meant making them miserable first. God, how she and Susan and Dan laughed together about Mom's latest antics. But, all that aside, she absolutely had to stop her mom's holy quest to find a suitable husband for her baby.* Julie tried, yet again, to make her mother understand.

"Mom, I'm not getting contacts. And you need to join the twentieth century. Women have careers. Marriage and kids just get put off for a while, that's all. It'll happen for me, too. I promise. You're just worried because I'll be thirty this year. That's what started all this, isn't it?"

Ida clasped her hands together. "Oh, I suppose. But, sweetie, if only you'd look for a man. Just date. But you won't. So, what choice do I have? Is it so much to ask that, before I die, I can be sure you have someone to love and care for you?"

"I don't need a man to care for me, Mother. I can do that myself. Besides, you're only fifty-seven. You're not going to die."

"I most certainly will…one day. Besides, I haven't been feeling well lately. I—"

"Bull. You'll outlive us all."

"Such language. It's unladylike, and men don't like it."

Julie grinned evilly at her mother, knowing just how to get to her. "Sure they do. Especially in bed."

Ida stood up. "If you're going to talk like that, then I'm just going to go home." She looked at her watch. "Your father should be back from golfing about now. I bring you a nice man, and this is the thanks I get."

Julie jumped up and came around the couch to put her hands fondly on her mother's shoulders. "I didn't ask you to bring me a man. And he's the fourth one this month. But this guy is an FBI agent. Don't be surprised if they show up at your door and haul you off. Or maybe they'll have your taxes audited every year for the next twenty years, Mom."

"The IRS does that. But didn't you think he was nice?"

Julie opened her mouth, closed it, and then tried again. "Yes, I did. Very nice. Especially under the circumstances. But that's not the point, Mother."

"Good, because I thought he was, too. And such a handsome man. Now, with any luck, your bank will be robbed and he'll be assigned the investigation. Wouldn't that be wonderful?"

"The bank being robbed would be wonderful?"

Ida made an impatient noise. "No, of course not. Seeing Mike again would be wonderful."

A sudden terror swept over Julie. "Mom, you wouldn't go so far as to arrange a bank heist, would you?"

A huge bulb of an idea appeared over Ida's head and lit her face. But it dimmed just as suddenly. "No. That wouldn't work. Too many details."

Julie threw her hands up in the air and started pacing the length of her bright living room. "All right, you win! I give up. I swear to you I will resume dating, forget my job, forget the promotion I want and find a husband. There! Are you happy now?''

"Find a husband? What's wrong with the one I brought you?''

Julie stopped pacing and conceded defeat. "Nothing. Nothing's wrong with him. The man is gorgeous—''

"So, you think he's gorgeous? I did do well this time, didn't I? See? I told you I could pick you a prince.''

Julie thought about that. *A prince? Boy, no kidding.* "All right, fine. I'll marry him. There. Are you happy? Now will you stop putting ads in the personals and setting up interviews at the mall?''

Her mother had the grace to look chagrined. "Those were disasters, weren't they?'' Looking everywhere but at her daughter, Ida walked over to get her purse from the glass-and-brass dining room table. She pulled out a letter. "This is from Susan. She's been to her obstetrician again, and her letter's just full of baby news. I thought you'd want to read it.''

Husbands and babies. Her mother's world. Julie's heart softened. "What am I going to do with you, Mom?''

Ida pulled her world-famous pouting face. "Well, I just want you to be happy. Like Dan and Susan are in their marriages. Is that so terrible?'' She plopped the letter on the table.

But Julie wasn't sucked in. Instead, she pictured her older brother and sister, who would be laughing about now. "Dan lives in Maryland and Susan in California. Do you think it's an accident that they fled Florida, Mom?''

"They didn't flee anything. Dan was transferred to Baltimore, and Ben took that teaching job in San Francisco, so what choice did Susan have but to follow him? That's what wives do.''

"I wouldn't know.'' She was already cringing when the words hit the air. No, no, no…

"Which brings us back to why I'm here.''

2

"IT'S FRIDAY AFTERNOON, Mike, and you're just now telling me that some crazy lady last Saturday says you need to meet her daughter, then grabs your kid's hand and hauls the two of you to *her* kid's apartment. Then she introduces you to this gorgeous redhead and says the two of you should get married? You sat on that for a week? Man! Why don't things like that ever happen to me?"

Mike filled his mug with coffee and placed the glass pot back on its burner. Looking over at his partner, pug-nosed and sporting a crew cut, he grinned. "Things like that don't happen to you because you're so damned ugly, Sal. Mamas take one look at you and see ugly grandkids. Nobody wants ugly grandkids."

"Yeah, yeah, and the horse you rode in on, DeAngelo. So, how come you didn't say nothin' until today?"

"Hell, I don't know. Nothing else to talk about by Friday, I guess. It's not like it's big news."

"Are you kiddin' me here? News? It's headlines, Mikey. Headlines. A gorgeous redhead handed to you on a silver platter—by her mother? And you don't think it's news? I thought I raised you better than that."

Mike grinned. When Sal was excited, his Brooklyn accent thickened. "You sure don't talk like a fed, Agent Pomerantz."

"Hey! I was from Brooklyn before I was FBI, cowboy. Like you and Oklahoma. It's in the blood, you know? So, you gonna tell this chick about Caroline?"

A sudden stab of...something...pricked at Mike, making

him sound more abrupt than he'd intended. "Her name's Julie. And it doesn't matter about Caroline, because I'm not going to see her again."

Sal's feet and chair came down in simultaneous thumps. "You're yanking my chain here. You and Caroline on the outs or something? And here I thought you and she were like this…this perfect couple."

"Man, pay attention. Not Caroline. Julie. I won't be seeing Julie again."

Sal sat back. "Oh, Julie. My mistake. So, can I have Julie? I like gorgeous redheads as much as the next guy."

Refusing to rise to the bait, Mike ignored Sal's hooting laughter. Sipping at his coffee, he went to stare out the single window in their cramped office. Not even the thought of picking up Caroline at the airport could hold his attention today.

Distracting him instead were the same thoughts that had kept him preoccupied all week. Thoughts of one cute-as-hell redhead about ten miles away in Brandon. Who hadn't been wearing a bra. Or shoes. And who had a crazy mother. Talk about crazy—that was Life with a capital *L*. You think you're all set, and then—bam. There she is—the woman of your dreams. Only she's not the girl who's wearing your ring. Mike shook his head, like he was the butt of this huge cosmic joke.

Wait just a—what the hell was he thinking? Woman of his dreams? He glanced quickly at Sal, half-afraid he'd spoken his thoughts aloud. No, Sal was busy scribbling something in his journal. Relieved, Mike turned away from the window and went to sit at his cluttered desk. He set his mug on a manila folder, looked at the ream of paperwork waiting to be dealt with, and immediately stood up again.

Sal banged his hand down on his desk, startling Mike. "If you don't quit pacing around like some kinda animal, DeAngelo, I'm gonna throw you out that window myself. What's eating you? You missing your sweetie or what?"

"Hell, no." Mike frowned, knowing he'd lose several

macho points if he ever admitted to something as sentimental as missing his fiancée. Sitting back down, he ducked
his head to keep Sal from seeing the secret smile that stole
over his features when he pictured Caroline. The woman
he loved and was going to marry in two months. Caroline.
That was who he needed to think about.

Probably what he loved best about Caroline, he decided,
was that she wasn't anything at all like Victoria. Thinking
about his ex-wife deepened Mike's frown. Life to Tory was
like some damned smorgasbord laid out before her, and all
she had to do was nibble each moment before moving on
to the next dish. The sad part was, being a wife and a
mother had been nothing more to her than the next thing
to be tasted. Well, he hoped she was happy now, globe-
trotting for that fancy travel magazine. Thank God for Caroline. He was lucky to have her. She was warm, sweet,
loving and committed to Aaron and him. Just as he was
committed to her.

Having lightened the load on his heart considerably,
Mike turned to his partner. "You know what, Sal? For the
first time since I've known you, I think you're right. I must
be missing Caroline. Otherwise, I probably wouldn't have
noticed a redhead with legs up to her neck."

Sal frowned. "Hey, don't take this love thing too far,
Oklahoma. You're engaged, is all. So, if ever you don't
notice a gorgeous woman, I'll say nice things about you at
the funeral. Because you'll be dead."

Mike grinned. "All right then, to prove I'm not dead,
did I tell you about this funny thing Julie said? She yanked
her mother into her apartment and closed the door. And
then she opened it again and—" He clammed up instantly
when Sal's expression became purely mocking.

Sal pushed back in his swivel chair and put his feet up
on his metal desk. "So-o-o-o, tell me again about the
woman you're engaged to marry? The one you're picking
up this very night at the airport and escorting tomorrow

night—Saint Valentine's Day, no less—to some family out-
ing? Tell *me,* your future best man, about *her.*"

Mike pulled a face and tugged at his knotted tie. "Aren't
you the one who said it doesn't cost anything to look?"

"There! You did that thing again with your tie. You
know you do that every time I mention Caroline or you
gettin' married?"

Mike frowned. "Do what?"

"You pull at your tie and loosen your collar. Like they're
choking you."

Mike stared at him. "The hell I do."

"The hell you don't."

"The hell I do."

"Okay. Have it your way." Sal grinned and stared. Then
he blurted, "Caroline!"

Mike caught himself as his hand went to the knot at his
throat. He scowled, which had no effect on Sal's riotous
laughter. "Knock it off, Pomerantz."

Sal held his hands up. "Okay, okay. I'm on your side,
Mikey. It ain't like I'm the one always talking about honor
and commitment. That's your life."

Mike scowled. "Damn straight it is. Because those are
two things my ex-wife never felt, not even for Aaron. Her
job was always more important than her family. It came
first every time. And from the little I know about Julie,
she's the same way. But not Caroline. Caroline will always
be there for Aaron."

"And for you," Sal added softly. "Eh, Mikey?"

Mike looked at his partner and then looked down at the
work on his desk. "Yeah, for me, too." Then, after a moment of silence, he turned to Sal. "Don't you have something you need to be doing, Pomerantz, besides sticking
your nose into my life?"

Sal leaned back in his chair, knotting his fingers together
behind his head. "I got the same as you—squat. Just
pushin' paper."

Mike grimaced his agreement, then picked up a file and

opened it. Turning to Sal, he gave him his best Defender of Freedom face. "If you wanted adventure, young man, you should have joined the navy. This is the FBI, where we have to wait around until the bad guys rob banks or something."

"Yeah, well, they're overdue. Damn criminals. Can't depend on nobody anymore. But at least we're not stationed in Milwaukee or Detroit. If I have to be bored, then the view may as well be good. It's the middle of February, and we got sunshine and beaches and women. Can't complain."

Sunshine and beaches and women. Mike stared at the file in front of him, but the image of that damned pixie face and red hair played through his mind instead. He smiled. Can't complain.

"WELL, I'M GLAD YOU THINK it's funny, Susan. I was so embarrassed, I could have died. You're safely married—and pregnant again. And on the other side of the continent. So you've forgotten what Mom's like." Julie kicked off her heels and began unbuttoning her suit jacket. She balanced the telephone receiver between her jaw and her shoulder.

"What? Sorry. I'm undressing. Well, because the phone was ringing when I walked in from work. Okay, wait a minute." She put the receiver down to yank off her short-sleeved jacket and slim skirt. And then her bra and panty hose. Ah, heaven.

Clad only in her underpants, she sat cross-legged on her bed and put the phone back to her ear. "Okay, I'm back. Yeah, I'm picking you up at the airport tomorrow. Yes, arrival time…gate number…and the airline—got 'em. Susan, I'll be thirty in September, and I'm a lending officer at one of the biggest banks in Florida. Who just happens to be up for a vice presidency. All that adds up to me being a responsible adult. Oh, shut up. Career, career, career. I know. Huh? Oh, please—not the biological clock thing again. You're beginning to sound like Mom. Hah! Thought that'd scare you.

"Hey, is Tommy excited about his upcoming airplane ride?" She listened for a moment and then laughed. "The little turkey. I can't wait to see him. It will be so much fun tomorrow night. Or a complete nightmare, considering all the relatives here for Nana's eighty-fifth birthday. I know! I can't wait to see y'all, either. Yeah, Dad's picking up Dan and Joan tonight. Okay, I'll let you go. Give Ben and Tommy my love. Bye."

After hanging up the receiver, Julie straightened her legs out and fell backward on the bed. Closing her eyes, she lay unmoving, trying not to think. Could it be that her family was right and she was wrong? Would she regret her decision to have a career first, before marriage and children? She thought about her life. Well, aside from a little loneliness, she was pretty happy with things. And she'd be a heck of a lot happier if she got that promotion.

She had to admit it was looking pretty good. If she got it, she'd be the first woman to break into the upper management ranks at First Southern Bank. All the women were pulling for her, telling her how proud they were and how she would be setting a precedent for future women executives.

Future women. Julie put a hand over her belly, feeling its poochiness from her period, which had started today. On Friday the thirteenth. Appropriate. She made a face. This whole biological process of being a woman wasn't all that much fun. But necessary, she supposed. Almost unwittingly, she moved her fingers around in small circles, wondering what it would feel like to have a life growing inside her. Suddenly she grew wistful. Who said she couldn't have a career and a family? Women did it all the time nowadays. She just had to find the right man.

The Hunk's face popped into her mind. No, no more Hunk. He had a name—Mike. *Okay, go away, Mike.* But he wouldn't, so she forced her mind onto other things. Like how tired she was. The whole week had been hectic. And what if she'd come home tonight to kids and a husband and cooking and Little League and—no way. Lying here half naked and giving in to her fatigue may be selfish, but it was also much more satisfying.

There, she was thinking about something else. Until some evil little hussy inside her head remarked, *Yeah, and especially tiring had been trying to catch a glimpse of the Hunk around the complex.* Julie argued with her conscience. *Like there weren't ten separate three-story buildings with about a zillion units in each one. And all she knew was his first name. She couldn't even check out the mailboxes.* Suddenly, Julie opened her eyes. What was she thinking? God, she was turning into a stalker. *Like mother, like daughter.*

Scary thought. Smirking at herself, she continued lying there, looking at the ceiling, absentmindedly picturing Mike's face, until a heavy-handed banging on her front door startled her. What in the world? Some man was calling out her name.

"Coming!" Quickly she grabbed her terry-cloth robe from the foot of the bed and put it on, tying the belt securely. Padding down the hallway to the door, she mentally ran through the short list of men she knew who could possibly be banging on her door on a Friday afternoon. Curious. Not for the first time, she wished she had a peephole in her door. "Hello? Who is it?"

"Julie, thank God. It's me—Mike DeAngelo. Open up."

Mike DeAngelo? She didn't know any Mike—Mike DeAngelo! So that was his last name. She looked down at herself. No! "Uh, wait a minute, Mike. I'm not dressed. Let me—"

"Julie, open up. There's no time. Aaron left the apartment, and I can't find him. I think he went outside when I was in the shower—"

Julie unlocked the door and jerked it open, feeling the cool rush of evening air on her face. "What happened?"

Mike looked wild, frantic. His hair was wet, and he was wearing a pair of blue jeans—and that was all. His hands were tucked under his armpits. "I guess he's not here?"

"No. Of course not. Come in. You must be freezing."

"I'm okay, but I can't come in. I have to find him. I cannot believe he did this."

"Come in and let me change clothes. I'll help you look. Tell me what happened."

He looked at her as if he'd just suddenly realized where he was. "All right. But hurry."

"Ten seconds—tops." He stepped inside, and Julie closed the door behind him. "Talk to me while I change." She didn't wait for an answer, but ran down the hallway to her bedroom, untying her robe as she went.

"I got in from work and was changing clothes," he called down the hallway. "I laid out some clean clothes for him and a snack, and told him to sit at the table with it. Man, this is a mess. We're supposed to be at the airport in less than two hours."

"I'm listening," Julie called out when he paused. She thrust her legs into her fat pants—an old pair of sweats—and yanked them up.

"Anyway, he came into my room and said he wanted to see that grandma-lady's girl again—"

"Who? Ohmigod—my mother. This is all my fault!" She tied the waist strings into a loose bow and hustled to her dresser, jerking open a drawer and grabbing the first T-shirt she found.

"It's not your fault. He's wanted to come see you all week, but I wouldn't bring him."

Julie stopped in the middle of pulling on her shirt. *So, why wouldn't you bring him to see me, Mike?* She pulled the shirt over her head and tugged it down. "Go on. I'm almost ready."

"He was watching cartoons while I took a shower. I thought I heard the door when the water was running, but figured it was probably his bedroom door. Anyway, when

I was drying off, I went to check on him. And he was gone. God, I can't believe this! Why didn't I use the damned safety chain?''

''We'll find him, Mike.'' At her closet now, Julie kicked aside her tennis shoes and dug around for her slip-on sandals. No time for shoelaces. Finding them, she plunged her feet into them, and then bounded back to the living room.

Rounding the corner, she ran into Mike. She reached out to catch herself, landing her hand on his bare chest. He took hold of her arms to steady her. She froze for just an instant, aware of the contact and of the warm, hard feel of him. ''Don't worry, Mike. We'll find him. And he'll be fine. I promise you.''

Staring up at him, she pronounced herself glad that the glint of rage reflected in his black eyes wasn't meant for her. ''I hope to God you're right, Julie.''

''I am, Mike. I just know it.'' Still, the look on his face and his tight grip on her arms made her glad she was on his side. She managed to nod her head at him. ''Let's go.''

He looked down at her chest, blinked and looked again. ''I'm a virgin, but this is a very old shirt.''

''What?'' Then she looked down at herself. Oh, geez. He was reading her shirt's message. ''Um, it's old, and I wasn't paying attention to what…I…'' She looked up at him, lost in her embarrassment.

''It's okay.'' Then he looked at his grip on her arms and let go of her quickly. ''I've hurt you.''

''No, you didn't. You're just upset. Let's go.'' She went to the door and opened it, turning to see if he was following her. He was hot on her heels. In fact, he was past her and out of the apartment in three long strides.

Julie closed the door behind her and sprinted to catch up with him. She stopped next to him as he stood looking at Providence Road, off to their right. As usual, it was alive with cars zipping by. And traffic on Brandon Boulevard, less than a quarter mile north, made the Indianapolis 500 look like a tortoise race. He didn't have to tell her what he was thinking. No child would stand a chance out there.

To gain his attention, she put her hand on his bare arm. His muscles jumped at the contact, and he turned to look down at her. "He's fine, Mike. Just keep thinking that. He's probably home right now watching cartoons again. Let's go check there first."

He nodded and took off at a lope, heading south through the myriad of moss-draped oaks that ringed the grounds. Being barefoot was not a problem for him, apparently, because he fairly zipped by and around the cars parked in front of the blue-painted stucco buildings. Almost immediately, he left her behind, disappearing around the corner of an adjacent building.

The man must be part gazelle, Julie groaned. With her hands cupped under her braless and swollen breasts to support them, she jogged after him, trying to keep up and keep her leather sandals on all at the same time. Her respect for FBI conditioning rose four or five notches as she caught sight of Mike ahead. He was methodically zigzagging his way through the maze of buildings that comprised the complex, looking everywhere for any sign of his son.

At the last building, just as Julie staggered up, breathing heavily and clutching the wall for support, Mike entered the first breezeway and jerked open a door, calling out, "Aaron! You in here, buddy?"

With one hand to her pounding heart, she focused on his tormented expression and listened with him. After several long seconds, during which Julie realized Mike was barely winded, they exchanged a glance. Nothing.

"Where have you looked, Mike?"

"Everywhere. The pool, the sauna. The gym. Tennis courts. The office. The trash Dumpsters. Your place. Everywhere."

Julie grimaced in frustration. That was everywhere. "Does he have any little friends who live nearby?"

Mike shook his head. "No. The poor kid's never home.

It's late when I pick him up. He stays in Tampa with the wife of an agent and their kids during the day. So, no, there's just him and me. And you.''

An unexpected thrill leapt through her at being included in his circle. Then she had a dashing thought. "What about his mother, Mike? Where's she? Would he try to go to her?"

He pulled a face. "No, she's hang-gliding in Holland, as usual. It's just been me and Aaron for most of his life. He knows he can't find her around here.''

So he's divorced. But hang-gliding in Holland? As usual? Would he tease her at a time like this? "I hate to say it, but it's going to be dark soon. What should we do?''

He looked at her, at the evening sky, and then swore softly, leaning his bent arm against the doorjamb, using it as a rest for his forehead. Julie bit at her bottom lip. Never before had she felt so sorry for anyone in her whole life.

With her heart full, she moved to him, touching his arm in a tentative gesture of sympathy. Mike startled her by grabbing her and holding her crushed against him. Molded to him, unnerved by the sheer rightness of being in his arms, as well as by the sheer strength in his body, Julie pressed her cheek against the muscled wall of his bare chest. Black, crisp and curling hairs tickled her nose, as did the scent of his exertion and his fear. *God, please let us find his son,* she prayed.

"Look what I found, Daddy.''

Julie froze—had she really heard that precious little voice?—and then pulled back to see Mike's face. He stared down at her, the same question in his eyes. Then, whipping around in reaction, they faced the speaker. Right behind them stood Aaron, holding up the biggest, ugliest frog Julie had ever seen. Mike released her and went down on his knees to hug his son's stocky little body to him. Hoarse, muffled utterances came from Mike as he pressed his face into Aaron's chubby little neck.

Julie had all she could do to keep from sobbing aloud.

She didn't even remember putting her hands to her mouth, but there they were. She took several gulping breaths and shook uncontrollably. *Thank you, God.*

Mike pulled back from Aaron, held him by his arms and looked him over, turning him around, running his hand over the boy's dark hair and grimy little face. "Where did you go, son? You scared the life out of me. Haven't I told you not to leave the apartment without telling me?"

Julie wrenched in a huge breath at the rasping sound of Mike's voice. She watched as Aaron started to say something, but then he spied her. His face lit up. "Look, Daddy, it's that grandma-lady's girl. Can I show her my frog?"

Still holding on to his son, Mike pivoted, bringing one knee up so his weight was on the ball of that foot. He smiled at her and shook his head, relief making him look vulnerable, somehow. Then he turned back to his son. "Yeah, big guy, you can. And then we're going to have a long talk. Do you understand that you scared me and Julie? We were very afraid for you."

Aaron's mouth puckered and his chin trembled. "I'm sorry, Daddy. I wanted to see the grandma-lady's girl, but I couldn't find her. An' then I couldn't find our 'partment. An' then I saw this froggy by the trees back there. An' I was playin' wif him. An' then—" That was as far as he got before he began wailing aloud.

Mike hugged his son to his bare chest again and scooped him up. As he stood, he soothed his child's belated fears. "It's okay. Daddy's right here. I love you, son. It's all right now. Here, show Julie your frog."

Now, Julie had never been a particular fan of frogs, but she loved this one. Smiling at Mike, she stepped up and stroked its head with a fingertip. Yep. Cold and wet. Gross. "Why, he's beautiful, Aaron. He really is. And we're so glad you're okay."

"Me, too." He turned to his father. "Can I keep him?"

Mike laughed. "Sure. You can keep him."

Aaron's face lit up. "Can we eat at Donnal-Macs?"

Mike translated for Julie. ''McDonald's.'' Then, turning to Aaron, he said, ''Sure. We can eat there.''

On a roll now, Aaron went on. ''Can Julie come wif us?''

Well, neither one of them had been expecting that. When Mike looked at her, Julie could see this was clearly a dilemma for him. Time for her to jump in. ''Thanks, Aaron, but I better not, honey. Another time, okay? I think you and your daddy have to go to the airport. Don't you want to see all the big airplanes?''

Mike was watching her—she could see him out of the corner of her eye. But not for anything could she look at him.

''Uh-huh. I like airplanes. They go fast—like this.'' He zoomed the pop-eyed frog around in circling motions in the air. ''Me and Daddy's goin' to get Caroline. I have to be nice to her 'cause her's going to be my new 'nother mommy.''

3

JULIE SHOULD HAVE BEEN ecstatic. After all, she was thankfully related to all these people here at Nana's birthday party on Valentine's Day. "Thankfully," because that meant her mother couldn't fix her up with any of the single men present. Yes, she had every reason to be happy, but she wasn't.

Darn it, she hadn't set out to be miserable. It'd just turned out that way. Oh, Nana's party was a huge success, all right. The old dear loved being the center of attention. Julie chuckled, thinking of her grandmother's face when everyone jumped out to surprise her. It was nice to have one's advanced age remarked on by huge crowds, as she'd so eloquently put it.

Given the festive circumstances, Julie owned up to the fact that she was the only flop tonight. That was why she'd taken off to be alone when the band took a break. Having danced with everyone present at least once, she now sat in a corner of the brightly lit and streamer-decorated country club ballroom with her shoes off, a plate of food in her lap, and her self-pity on her proverbial sleeve.

Sighing, she swung her feet up onto the next chair. The milling, chattering, laughing crowd of her relatives, most of whom she wouldn't have recognized if she'd passed them on the street, only managed to irritate her. What did they have to be so happy about?

No. That wasn't fair. And, okay, she was certainly thrilled to see her brother and sister and their families again. But everyone and everything paled next to her blue funk over learning last evening that some Caroline-chick was going to be Aaron DeAngelo's new 'nother mommy.

Worse, she had no rational reason to be upset about it. But Mike was supposed to marry her. Just ask her mother. An unladylike snort escaped her. Well, she'd said no rational reason. Julie looked down at her plate and gave up pretending she was eating any of the food on it. Wrinkling her nose, she twisted just enough to set it down on the floor.

In a full-blown pout now, she straightened up and crossed her arms under her breasts. To hell with being sociable. She felt more like getting stinking drunk and brawling with some big, burly bikers. Like she did *that* every weekend. For several moments, lost in that vision, she glared a challenge to the far wall. Getting no fight there, she looked down at her lap.

Well, just great. Crumbs and more crumbs. God, she was such a pigpen. She began gingerly flicking them off the short skirt of her black-and-white cocktail dress. Oh, even better. That one wasn't a crumb. Now she'd managed to make an abstract painting out of a dot of mustard on the white pattern in her skirt. Looking at the yellow smear, she rolled her eyes. Typical. Maybe club soda would take it out.

She looked up. No way. The bar was on the other side of the crowded room. An image of encountering her mother and having her trying to remove the stain with an old tissue from her purse and saliva kept Julie firmly in place. Okay, next best thing. Mental calculations told her that the powder room was right around the corner from where she was sitting. Aha, with cold water and a paper towel, she ought to be able to create a water stain huge enough to detract from the mustard.

Quirking her mouth up in self-deprecation, she swung her feet down and looked around the room. No one was paying the least bit of attention to her. Good. She'd just leave her shoes there and slink around the corner. Gathering her flared skirt in her hands, Julie ducked her head and skittered the short distance to the rest-room door. Using her hip to push against it, she backed into the room and turned around.

Mike and Aaron DeAngelo stood side by side, facing the tiled wall in front of a low, metal trough-thingy, apparently…taking care of business.

Stunned, Julie sucked air for a full ten seconds before giving herself away. "Mike!"

He looked up. And froze. "Julie! What the—"

Aaron proved to be more eloquent. "Look! It's that grandma-lady's girl another time! She's in the boys' pee-pee room!"

Julie whispered roughly. "Mike, what are you doing here?"

He looked around pointedly, then giving each word the same attention, said, "You mean in the men's room?"

"The men's room?" Julie's blood ran cold. She gave her surroundings the once-over. Totally alien landscape. The men's room. *Run.* Yet her feet remained rebelliously frozen to the floor. She suspected the heated flush on her cheeks was better than a neon sign that blinked "Female Intruder, Female Intruder."

Two sets of male eyes continued to stare at her. By her own calculations, she had two options. She could run now and live out her remaining years in the back of her closet. Or she could brazen it out and make them think they were in the wrong. She voted for option number two. "Not the men's room. What are you doing *here?*"

Mike and Aaron, otherwise engaged but still managing to look somewhat like deer caught in the headlights, both stared at the floor where she was pointing. Men could be so obtuse, even the baby ones.

Julie stomped her bare foot. "Not the floor. Here. At this club, Mike. We rented the whole thing for Nana's party. You know—my family? What are you doing here?"

"Your party? The Charlotte Nelson birthday party is your party? She's your grandmother?"

"Is your grandma-lady here, too, Julie?"

She looked at Aaron. "Yes." She looked at Mike. "Yes."

The door behind her swung open. "Whoa. Wrong room. Sorry, Julie."

She jerked around in time to see Dan ducking out. The door closed. It opened again almost immediately. Again it was Dan, and he was already unzipping. He went straight to that trough-thingy with Mike and Aaron, and proceeded with the matter at hand. "Dammit, Julie, I almost went in the— Wait a minute. That means you're— What're you doing in the men's room, baby sister? Has Mom reduced you to checking out guys' packages in here?" His expression faded. "Mom's not in here, is she?"

Julie shook her head.

"Thank God." He looked over at Mike and Aaron. "Evening. I don't normally talk to men at a urinal, but I assume we're related. How you doing? I'm Dan Cochran— the cute-but-crazy woman here's older brother. I guess you two've met?" He kept one hand on his business, but held out his other one to Mike.

Julie watched Mike's eyes glaze over. Then, with one deft movement, he turned his back to her, adjusted his...stuff, zipped up and turned back around. "Yeah, I know her. I'm Mike DeAngelo. This is my son, Aaron. And we're not related." But gentleman that he was, he shook Dan's hand.

"You're not related to your son?" Dan asked it in all good-natured, blond, blue-eyed innocence. To the naked eye, anyway.

Julie, still stood rooted to the spot, managed not to flinch when Mike looked from Dan to her, as if to say this was all her fault, and then back to Dan. "Yes. Of course I'm related to my son. And, no, I'm not related to you. Or your sister. For which I will daily thank God."

Dan let loose with the famous Cochran laugh that echoed in a hee-hawing manner through the hallowed halls of the men's room. The cacophony startled Aaron into grabbing his father's leg. He wasn't the first small child to be undone by that sound. Julie watched as Mike bent to help the boy make himself decent.

And somehow that sight gave her the courage to turn tail and run. With her arm out in front of her, she pushed into the door, only to realize it opened inward and that she'd nearly broken her arm. She backed up, jerked on the metal handle, opened it and peeked outside. The coast was clear. She made a mad three-step dash for the door across the tiny vestibule, the door clearly marked Ladies Room.

Oh, sure, now it was obvious. Once inside, she leaned her back against it and brought her hand up to her chest, as if that gesture could make her heart quit pounding.

Almost immediately, someone on the other side of the door pushed against it. With a yelp, Julie jumped away and turned around. In walked Federal Agent Mike DeAngelo, looking every bit as serious as a search warrant.

"Mike! What are you doing in here?" She looked around frantically. There was nobody here but them—at least out here in the large, civilized sitting area with all its mirrors and delicate furniture and long vanity. No telling about the private stalls around the corner, though.

"What am I doing in here? I think you've lost your right to ask that question. Now, what in the hell is going on?"

"Where's Aaron?"

That stopped him. For about a second. "He wanted to see your mother. Your brother's taking him to her. I assume he's sane—your brother, not Aaron. I know he's sane."

"He's sane. He's an airline pilot."

There followed a moment of weighted silence. "Those two things don't always go together, Julie."

It took her a moment to realize that he was again advancing on her. "What are you doing?" She tried to back up. There was no place to go. Her heart pounded against her ribs.

Then he was right in front of her. And taking hold of

her arms. "What am I doing? I'm probably making the biggest mistake of my life, but I've been wanting to do this since the first moment I saw you. And I sure as hell hope you want me to, because—"

And then he kissed her. Full on the mouth. With a ton of heat and passion and swirling tongues and heavy breathing. Stunned, but realizing he was right—she did want him to kiss her, Julie melted into his arms. Thrilled from her scalp to the bottoms of her feet, she put everything she had into returning his kiss.

Just the very rightness of being in his arms was what finally struck a chord in the functioning part of her mind. That, and the ecstasy of feeling him molded to her from lips to toes, making her happy she was a woman. *Whoa, this man was the man for her. To heck with that Caroline chick. Let her get her own. Oh, God, he was her own.*

Julie's eyes opened. Her vision was filled with tall, dark, handsome and incredibly-good-kisser-for-an-FBI-agent Mike DeAngelo. She pushed him away. Or tried to. She only succeeded in pushing herself backward. Wiping at her lips, she watched him put his hands to his waist. One dip of her gaze down his black slacks revealed he was glad he'd kissed her. Either that, or he had a gun stuffed down his pants.

Cut to the chase, girl. "Who's Caroline?"

He slumped a little bit. So did "it." Well, she couldn't help but notice. Locking his black-eyed gaze on her and speaking gravely, he intoned, "She's my fiancée."

Julie swallowed hard, ignoring the lump in her throat. "I know she's your fiancée. I meant, to me—what is Caroline to me? Everyone here is my family, Mike. Do you realize what that means? Heck, do you realize what this—" she flapped her hand in the air between herself and him "—means?"

He ran a hand through his hair as he looked everywhere but at her. Then he stepped back, sitting on the low vanity behind him. "I don't know what she is to you. Her last

name is Wyndemere. And that's a pretty far stretch from
Nelson or Cochran.''

Julie sat down heavily. Good thing there was a chair
behind her. ''Wyndemere? Of the Boston Wyndemeres?''

Mike nodded. ''The very same.''

''This is not good. Caroline Wyndemere. You have got
to be kidding me. Mom has talked about her before like
she's some kind of crown princess. She's my Nana's oldest
sister's youngest son's third granddaughter, or something
like that. Anyway, she's beautiful, blond, and the darling
of the rich side of the family. The really rich side.''

''That's my Caroline.''

Julie almost burst into tears. To hear him say—after having just kissed her—that she was *his* Caroline. Well, what
did she expect? He was engaged to marry her. Even so, she
made a conscious effort to keep her voice steady. ''So,
how'd you two meet?''

His face became all square angles and shadowed planes.
Clearly, he didn't want to talk about this. ''At a charity
benefit. Mutual friends.''

''Oh? Like who—the Vanderbilts or the Astors?''

The expression that hardened his face was probably one
he'd perfected for dealing with bad guys. ''This isn't getting us anywhere.''

''Oh, my mistake. Then, tell me this, how come this is
the first time I've seen you tonight? My humble family
tends to notice people who fly in on their own jets and then
arrive in limos. That is how she got you here, right?''

Mike let out a burdened breath. ''You don't even know
Caroline, and you've already judged her. But to answer
your question, we just got here. And yes, in a limo. We'd
have been here sooner, but we ran into some friends over
dinner—''

''She wouldn't even eat here with the riffraff, huh?''

He quietly observed her for a moment. Julie tried not to
squirm under such trained scrutiny. ''Don't be like that. It's
not attractive.''

Stung, she bristled to her full seated height. "Well, maybe I'm not trying to be attractive. Did you think about that? I mean, anyone who's barefoot and has mustard on her dress and barges into the men's room—"

"Is my kind of woman." As if his words alone weren't surprise enough, he grinned at her.

She looked down at her skirt and fiddled with it. *So, if I'm your kind of woman, what are you doing with Caroline?* No, she had no right to think that. *Says who?* He'd kissed her—that gave her the right. Still, taking three emotional steps back, she looked up at him. "We've got to quit meeting like this."

The smile was still there and was joined by a warm chuckle. "Yeah. We wouldn't want people to talk—any more than they're going to after this."

"Yeah, really. So, what are we going to do now?"

His gaze went to the plush, plump couch along the opposite wall. Julie's mouth dried. A thrill of warning went through her when she realized she was ready to race him for it. Never in her life had she ever felt such instant, just-let-me-get-my-hands-on-you longing for a man. Boy, had her mother picked one this time. Yeah—her cousin's fiancée.

"Do? Well," he pronounced with a certain finality, "I guess we ought to at least leave the powder room."

"Good plan." She'd meant what were they going to do about what they felt for each other. But his plan had merit, too, even if it was typically male and logical. And it made her mad. "So, once we're out there, we'll just pretend you never kissed me. And act like we don't know each other when we're introduced, and you're with your fiancée—my cousin. Lovely."

"Don't be like this. This is the last thing I expected to happen. I shouldn't have kissed you, and I'm sorry. I don't know what I was thinking. You just keep popping into my life when I least expect it. But it's my problem—I'm the one who's engaged."

Please, let's keep talking about your engagement. She covered her emotions by rolling her eyes and being snippy. "Oh, I know full well about your commitment. But don't worry—I don't think one kiss is a betrayal of anything sacred. We can tell people we're kissing cousins."

He narrowed his eyes. "Enough said on that. We ought to be concentrating on three things. One, your mother will never let us get away with pretending not to know each other. Two, your crazy brother is probably right now the center of attention while he adds another tale to your family history. And three, Aaron's probably told everyone outside this room about seeing the grandma-lady's girl in the boys' pee-pee room."

Those last words, coming out of his mouth, should have been funny, but they weren't. Not under these circumstances.

A disgusted groan accompanied her words. "All this because I dropped mustard on my skirt and you can't control your testosterone."

"What? Who says I can't control my testosterone?"

Ready with a definitive answer, Julie opened her mouth, but a flushing toilet caught her attention. A moment later, a beaming Ida Cochran came out from one of the stalls. "Well, I do, for one, Mike."

"Mother! You were in there listening all this time!" Julie was truly horrified.

"Mrs. Cochran!"

The queen mother, making her grand exit, inclined her head regally to each of them as she passed by. "Julie, my darling baby. Mike, my future son-in-law."

LESS THAN TEN MINUTES later, Julie amended her labeling of "the bathroom scene" as the worst moment in her life. It now held a firm second place to sitting at this gaily festooned, white-clothed table with her family and Mike and Caroline and having to listen to Dan's teasing recitation of her blundering into the men's room. She couldn't wait until

Julie Marie Cochran—will ever love and have his arm around her? And his ring on her finger? Was that fair?

Where had that come from? Julie stared into space for a moment and then chanced a look at Mike. He frowned right back at her. The only man she would ever love? When had that been decided? And by whom? Fighting her own epiphany, Julie forced herself into a nonchalant pose, resting an elbow on the table and supporting her chin with her hand. Thank God, Caroline was still holding court.

"It's so wonderful being here with all of you. I wish we'd done this years ago. Being an only child, well…I just love big families. All the hugging and laughter. I can't wait to start a family of my own." She turned cow eyes—in Julie's estimation—on her doting fiancé.

That did it. Julie clattered her fork onto her dessert plate, drawing everyone's attention. "Oops, sorry."

She made a face right back at Mike and enjoyed watching his face turn scarlet when everyone at the table stared at him, too. Hah.

Caroline smiled and looked nervously around. "Well, it wasn't really important. I was just saying that I hope we get to see one another more often. I'll have to remember to tell Reginald when I get back home—he didn't come with me this trip…." Caroline paused, her expression uncertain.

What's this? Julie focused her feminine radar and shifted her gaze to Mike. He looked ticked off. *So-o-o-o, Reginald was a sore spot, huh?* Julie looked back to Caroline, only to see her glance at Mike, who was now doing a stone-faced Mount Rushmore impression.

Poor old Caroline picked up the unraveling threads of her comment. "I'll tell Regi…him to pencil in visits for us all. It just seems that up until now, what with my living so far away, and with my work—"

Julie nearly choked on her coffee. "You work?"

Well, why was everyone looking at her as if she'd just pulled a plucked and squawking chicken out from under the table? She'd asked a simple question, for crying out loud. Setting down her cup, she narrowed her eyes at the reproachful stares trained on her by her brother and his wife, her sister and her husband, her father and Mike.

Once again, Caroline jumped in, speaking rapidly and drawing all eyes to her. "Yes, I do. Though, it's not a job, really, and nothing so vital as what you do, Julie. It's just that...Reginald seems to think I need more to occupy my time. It's more charity work, I suppose. Oh, now I'm embarrassed because it all sounds so...so self-serving."

When she looked uncertainly around the table, Jack Cochran leaned forward. "Oh, come on. We want to know. Tell us." Julie squelched an urge to hurl her wadded-up napkin at her father.

Caroline smiled timidly. *Man, this girl was not for Mike. He'd chew her up and spit her out inside of a year,* Julie was sure. Was she the only one who could see that? *Okay, Caroline, tell us all about it.*

"Well, if you're really interested." She gave them a plucky grin when they made polite noises of interest. "Oh, it's nothing. I volunteer my time for literacy, as well as doing work with an organization that helps unwed mothers. I also sit on the board of the Arts Council, and finance an after-school program for the disadvantaged youth in Boston. Those are the main ones."

"Damn, you're a regular Mother Teresa, aren't you?"

Julie wondered how Brother Dan liked being the one to replace her as the object of familial scorn. When she finished smirking at him, she bailed Caroline out. It was only fair. She really was a nice...timid person. And a relative. "I suppose you'll miss all that, once you and Mike are married and you and Reginald move here, right?"

"Oh, no," Caroline chirped brightly. "We're not—um, I'm not moving here. I couldn't possibly. Mike is resigning from the FBI, and we'll live in Boston."

"That hasn't been decided." Everyone, including a startled and chagrined Caroline, looked at Mike.

So, it really was possible to speak through clenched teeth. Leaning forward, Julie upped the ante. "Well, you're moving to Boston, Mike. Won't that be lovely? I guess if I'd thought about it, I would have realized that there'll be no need for you to work after you're married, right? You can stay home with Caroline and Reginald and Aaron all day. And, just think, you won't have to be Mr. FBI anymore. You can be Mr. M-O-M."

Mike glared a huge hole right through her. Julie grinned, actually enjoying this nasty streak of cattishness she hadn't known she possessed. *Well, darn it, she'd never wanted something this bad before. And she wasn't giving him up without a fight. Or without causing a fight, as the case may be.*

The band chose that moment to start up. Julie was sure she knew of one table that was glad they had. The familiar strains of "I Will Always Love You" filled the room with soulful sound. Just great. A song about always loving someone you can't have. Perfect for lovers and for slow dancing. What her father called a "buckle polisher." Julie's cattishness and taunting mood vanished. If Mike asked his fiancée to dance, she'd…she'd burst into tears.

And she nearly did when he leaned over to whisper something in his lover's ear. Caroline, the beautiful, blond cousin, turned smiling eyes up to her fiancé and nodded. Julie crunched her skirt mercilessly as she balled her hands into fists. And then she practically fell off her chair when Mike stood up and held his hand out. "Would you like to dance?"

Only he wasn't talking to Caroline. Or to Joan or Susan. He was talking to her. Julie. She said, "No."

Mike's handsome face went grim. "Yes, you would."

Someone—again to her left—pinched her side…hard. With a yelp, Julie was on her feet and glaring at her brown-haired sister-in-law, who just smiled sweetly back at her. Julie pointed at Joan, readying to share with her a particularly earthy suggestion, but then Mike grabbed her arm and led her, jerking futilely in his grasp, to a dark corner on the far side of the crowded dance floor.

Out of view of their table, he wrenched her into his arms, holding her as closely as possible without actually stuffing her in his pocket. But it was anger, and not tenderness, in his eyes. "Just what in the hell do you think you're doing, Julie?"

Struggling none-too-subtly to put some molecules of space between their bodies, she said tightly, "I don't know what you mean."

"Then, you're the only one who doesn't."

Julie looked up into his dark eyes and felt a staggering blow. Not a physical blow—just an awareness of something she'd thought earlier but hadn't actually absorbed until now. This man was truly the only man she would ever love. She would always love his stubborn jaw, his high cheekbones and fine, straight nose. And the feel of his trim, muscled body pressed to hers.

What was she going to do when he married her cousin? To Julie's utmost consternation, her body gave away her thoughts. Her chin quivered and tears gathered in her eyes. But still, she couldn't look away from his face, only inches from hers.

"Don't do it, Julie. Just…don't do it." With that, Mike pressed her head to his chest, turning her face away from the tables and toward the band. Exhaling sharply, he murmured, "Dammit."

She sniffed, blinking rapidly to clear the tears, and then closed her eyes. His hands on her turned exquisitely, painfully tender as he rubbed one hand up and down her bare back, exposed by the low cut of her dress. His other hand was pressed into the small of her back, holding her to him. Julie never hesitated, knowing this might be her only chance to embrace him. She slipped her hands inside his sports jacket and wrapped her arms around his torso, nestling into him as if they shared the familiarity of ten years of marriage. She breathed deeply of him, loving the scent of his after-shave and his own clean, male scent.

Julie closed her eyes, trying desperately to squeeze away fresh tears. A ragged sniff escaped her, threatening her control. But there was something she had to ask him and it couldn't wait. Pulling back from his embrace, she bit at her lip and gathered her courage. "Why did you kiss me?"

Mike slumped against her, as if he'd been preparing himself for this question. "I knew you were going to ask me that."

Looking up at him, Julie fell in love all over again with the chiseled nobility of his jaw and high cheekbones.

"I don't know, Julie. I don't know why I kissed you. I just had to."

She blinked and lowered her gaze to stare at a pearl button on his shirt. Raising her head again, she plunged in deeper. "Why? Why did you have to? I mean, it's obvious, after seeing you with Caroline, that you care for her."

His expression closed, became defensive. "Yes, I do."

Suddenly, her heart felt too heavy in her chest. "Then why, Mike? Why kiss me?"

He shifted and looked away, focusing on a point somewhere above Julie's head. She watched him, wanting with all her being to stroke the shadowed column of his neck and to smooth away the creases at the corners of his frowning mouth. When he looked back down at her, his soul was hidden. His black eyes were like mirrors that reflected only her. "I can't answer that."

"Can't? Or won't?"

"Can't."

Julie firmed her mouth, then let loose a hushed torrent of words. "What am I supposed to think? I think you're playing with me. It seems to me you're just getting pre-wedding jitters, and you have to have one last fling. But if I'm just a…a ripe field for your last wild oats, then I'll hate you forever, Mike DeAngelo."

Mike flinched and stepped back—onto the dance floor.

Two or three couples bumped into him. Mumbled apologies came his way, but were ignored as he glared down at her. "What kind of loser do you take me for?"

She didn't reply.

"Great. You're wrong, Julie. If you knew me better, you'd know that."

"Well, I don't know you better. It just seems to me that you couldn't kiss me like you did not twenty minutes ago, and then go sit by your fiancée, with your arm around her, and act like nothing happened, if you weren't a player."

For one instant, Mike stared at her as if she were something disgusting he'd found on the bottom of his shoe. "I don't need this garbage."

Then he turned and walked away, leaving her staring at his departing back.

4

"Ms. Cochran? I'm sorry to bother you, but…"

Julie looked up from the thick file in front of her that was giving her a killer Monday headache. Framed in the doorway of her crowded, second-floor office was Charlene, her executive assistant. When the woman noticed Julie's pained look, her expression fell.

"No, it's not you, Charlene. It's this convoluted loan application. What do you need?"

"For the record, *I* don't need anything, but *you* might want some aspirin. Your mother's here."

Julie clutched at her forehead. "No. Not today." It hadn't even been forty-eight hours since Nana's party, and the last thing she wanted was to answer questions about what had happened to make Mike and Caroline, not to mention her, leave so abruptly. She'd purposely not answered the phone all day yesterday, and boy, had it rung. "Don't we have security in this place? Or will they just let anyone in this bank?"

Charlene grinned. "Sorry."

Julie grimaced and went over her battle plan. "Okay, is she 'here' here, or downstairs meddling in the tellers' lives?"

"Downstairs meddling. This is an advance warning."

"Good. Tell her I died."

"I already did when I was down there a minute ago. She didn't buy it. Said it would've been in the paper, and she's already read the obituaries today."

"Great. Tell her I got transferred to Timbuktu."

Charlene frowned. "We have a branch there?"

"You're right. She wouldn't believe it. Then, I have no choice. I'll just have to kill her."

"I won't tell."

Julie laughed with her. Poor Charlene had a new hair color she hated and her kids were in a different day-care as a result of a ten-minute conversation with Ida Cochran last week.

"Oh, there's something else."

Julie arched an eyebrow. "You're killing me here."

"Sorry. I just thought you'd want to know that she's not alone."

Julie's stomach tightened. "Dear God, don't tell me she brought her bridge club up from Sun City Center again on a field trip? I swear she acts like coming to Brandon is open house at an elementary school. And wipe that grin off your face. You're enjoying this too much."

Charlene chuckled. "No. No bridge club. It's not even your father. It's some cute little tyke about three years old."

Now all of Julie's insides went cold. She'd kidnapped Aaron DeAngelo. Mike would call down the wrath of God on her demented mother. "Tell me, Charlene. What does this little boy look like?"

"Oh, he's so cute! He has blond hair and blue eyes, and he's carrying a teddy bear."

Julie nearly slumped over her desk in relief. "Thank God. It's Tommy, my nephew. My sister and her husband are here for the week. Wait. That explains it. I forgot she and Mom were coming up today for lunch. Did you notice if there was a blond, pregnant woman with her?"

Charlene shook her head and looked thoughtful. "I didn't see her. But the lobby's crowded. She could've been in the rest room, I guess. Anyway, I only spoke to your mom for a minute."

"Good thing. Otherwise, you might've had to sell your house and have your dog spayed."

"Yoo-hoo! Julie! We're here. Are you ready for lunch, sweetie?"

At the sound of her mother's voice in the foyer outside, immediately followed by the self-defensive closing of several office doors up and down the corridor, Julie and Charlene exchanged glances.

"You're on your own, boss."

"Coward." Julie pushed her leather chair back and stood up, calling out, "Come on in, Mom."

Charlene sidled out the doorway amid a flurry of introductions to Susan and Tommy, and I-told-you-so comments on how much better she looked as a brunette, as Ida swept in and hugged her baby to her. "Hi, sweetie. There's something wrong with your phone at the apartment. I called you all day yesterday and there was no answer. Oh, you look so grown-up and in-charge here. Doesn't she, Susan?" Ida turned to her older daughter. "See? Just like I told you—right there on the door, it says Senior Commercial Loan Officer. That is my baby. I just wish that picture of her downstairs was better." She turned back to Julie. "Honey, you should open your mouth more when you smile."

Julie copped a purposely droll face. "Hi, Mom. It's nice to see you, too."

"Oh, you know what I mean. Just overlook me. Well, can you go now? We thought we'd try that salad restaurant. All that roughage will be good for Susan's colon. It's important that pregnant women don't get constipated."

"Mother!" Julie's blond and beautiful sister put her hands to her flaming cheeks. "You have told that to everyone we've spoken to from your house to here—including the guy at the gas station and all the tellers downstairs."

Julie gave her older sister a sickeningly sweet smile. "Welcome home, sis. Do you remember now why you live in California?"

Julie hugged her older sister and then swooped Tommy and his teddy bear up into her arms to cover his little baby face with kisses. While he squealed and squirmed in her arms, she turned back to her mother, a smile on her face. But it instantly fled when a movement outside her office caught her eye. And held her attention.

Julie sucked in a breath. Her mother and Susan instantly sobered, as well, and turned abruptly in the direction Julie was staring. It was their turn to take surprised breaths. Standing in front of the closing elevator doors across the small foyer from them, and looking like an avenging angel, was Mike DeAngelo.

In a dark, tailored suit, white shirt and tie, he stood there, one knee bent, his hands in his pockets. He could have been posing for a men's wear layout. He also could have been chiseled out of granite, for all the warmth he exuded. His black-eyed gaze bore directly into Julie's, despite the intervening distance and the other people present.

Julie swallowed hard and tried her best to ignore her erratic heartbeat.

Ida was the first to find her voice. "Before you even think it, I didn't have anything to do with this."

Julie spared her mother a glance, but then her gaze sought Mike out again. He hadn't moved. She'd forgotten she was still holding Tommy until Susan helped him down from her arms.

"We'll wait downstairs, Julie. Come on, Mom. Come on, Tommy."

Julie thought she nodded her agreement, but she couldn't be sure. Suddenly, she felt as wooden as Pinocchio. And it was going to take more than a puppeteer to make her move her arms and legs.

Her family left her office and walked to the elevator. When they neared Mike, he smiled and spoke briefly to them, moving aside for them to pass. Once they'd boarded the elevator, her mother and Susan both turned will-you-be-okay? faces to her. Julie managed to raise a hand in a vague gesture that was meant to reassure them. Then the elevator doors closed.

She forced herself to swallow. Mike skirted the low

chairs and magazine-strewn tables in the waiting area to come stand at the door of her office. He stared at her without blinking. He looked so...professional. And impersonal. Well, he'd certainly paid attention the day they'd taught that look at the FBI academy.

When she began to sweat in earnest, she tried for a light tone. "Is this a personal or a professional call?"

He finally blinked. "Personal."

Her heart thudded. "Oh. So, I can assume we're not being robbed, or you haven't uncovered an embezzlement scheme?"

"No."

"'No, I can't assume,' or—"

"Knock it off, Julie." He dropped his federal agent pose to step inside and close the door behind him. Running a hand through his close-cropped hair, he paced within the small confines of her office. Then he stopped and faced her, his gaze flitting over her like she was some sort of enigma he had to solve. "I don't even know what I'm doing here. Caroline is still here and is at this minute with Aaron. And me? I'm supposed to be on my way to Plant City on a case. And, yet, here I am."

His uncertainty in her presence forced control into Julie's hands. She crossed her arms and shifted her weight to her other foot. "Maybe you came to apologize for Saturday night."

His response to that was to mumble a particularly descriptive curse as he slouched into the chair in front of her desk. Leaning back, he braced his elbows on the armrests and laced his fingers together. Then he looked her up and down. "All right. We can do this your way. I'm sorry about Saturday night."

Julie heated up like a simmering kettle. "Well, that sounded sincere. Do you even know what you're apologizing for?"

His eyelids drooped dangerously. "Why don't you tell me?"

She was glad to. "For kissing me when you had no right to, for one—"

"You didn't like it?"

She ignored his interruption. "And for leaving me standing there by myself like that, in front of all my relatives—"

"You insulted me."

"Oh, did I? And what did you do? You embarrassed me. You hurt me. You humiliated me. You—"

He was on his feet and holding her by her arms before she could finish her sentence. "Stop. You're right. All of it. I swear to God, I never meant to. I guess that's why I'm here. To tell you—" he shook his head slowly several times "—I never meant to hurt you."

Julie wondered if he could hear the roaring in her ears. No longer able to maintain eye contact with him, she looked off to the side, focusing on a three-drawer file cabinet in the corner. "Thank you for that much. I do believe you."

He exhaled and loosened his grip on her arms. She forced her gaze back to him. Well, she was glad she'd made him feel better. Too bad she didn't. Darn him, it would have been better for them both if he hadn't come today. Or ever again. If he felt such a need to apologize, he could have sent a card or flowers or left her a message on her answering machine. Her number was in the book. And he could have at least waited until his fiancée had left.

Then it hit her—right there while she stared up into his black eyes and watched him eyeing her mouth. Yes, her intuition told her, he could have done any of those things. But he hadn't. Because he'd wanted to see her again. It was that plain and simple.

But he was engaged to her cousin—a really nice woman, her conscience railed. Okay, she didn't think the rich girl was particularly suited to Mike, but that was none of her business. And he obviously cared enough about her to put a ring on her finger. All right, such was his life. What about hers? What about everything that was important to her—

her promotion and the late nights and weekend hours she was putting in on special bank projects she'd begun? Was she just going to trash all the months of hard work—for a man she couldn't have?

Put like that, her answer was simple. No. Well, then, if he wasn't strong enough to do the right thing, then, by golly, she was. And she'd do it now, before it got out of hand. Because the way he made her heart and body ache whenever she just thought about him, things could get out of hand—fast.

Hating herself for having a conscience, she took a deep breath and proceeded to break her own heart. Shrugging until he let go of her, Julie stepped back, pointedly going to her office door. It took every ounce of strength she possessed to remain upright and dry-eyed as she opened it. To anyone who might be passing her office, she hoped to give the impression of ending a simple business call. "Thank you, Mike, for coming by. I appreciate what you've done today. And I hope you and Caroline are very happy together."

She'd caught him off guard. For the briefest second, his surprise registered on his face. Then back came the federal agent look, the impersonal facade, the intent stare. But it hadn't quite gelled yet, because his mouth worked and he made a half gesture with his hands. Finally, though, he gave an accepting nod. "You're right. This is the only way. As I said before, I'm the one with the problem. Not you. Goodbye, Julie."

"Goodbye, Mike." She clutched at the doorknob behind her with both hands to keep from stopping him when he brushed by her. For the second time in less than two days, she watched him walk away from her. At least this time, it was on her terms. As if that made her feel any better.

When he reached the elevator, he punched the button and stood there, shaking his head. All the while, he kept his back to her, never once looking around.

When the doors didn't open immediately, he stalked to

the stairwell door and shoved it open. The door punched the wall behind it with a resounding bam as he stepped through. Office doors along the hallway opened in response to the noise. Concerned faces poked out. Julie eyed her co-workers and listened with them as Mike's footfalls descended rapidly down the stairs. The stairwell door slowly, anticlimactically closed behind him.

Julie blinked once. And then again. God, she hated Mondays.

A PIERCING, CHILDISH scream wrenched Mike out of his dozing nap and brought him straight up off the couch early Wednesday evening. Despite his fuzziness, a functioning part of his mind indicated reality for him. Okay, an hour ago, he and Aaron arrived home from seeing Caroline off at the airport. Aaron had fallen asleep on the way home, so when they got here, he'd put him in his bed and had hit the couch.

The scream echoed again, pitched high enough this time to clear Mike's sinuses. He pushed around the corner to Aaron's bedroom. Still clad in his overalls and T-shirt, the little boy sat on the floor with his legs spread wide. Between them was the old fish aquarium they'd converted into a frog-itarium. The lid was off it. And its only citizen had fled. Great. Now there was a fugitive frog loose somewhere in the apartment.

Mike ran his hands over his face to wake himself up and then stretched mightily. "What's up, hotshot? Was that you busting the sound barrier?"

Aaron turned a calm, serious face up to his father. "No. I was lellin' for you. I'm up from my nap now."

Mike smiled at the boy's tousled hair. "All the evidence points to that, Mr. DeAngelo. Now, what was all the yelling about?"

Aaron's chin quivered. "My froggy's gone. He got outta here."

Mike leaned against the doorjamb and crossed his arms

over his chest. "Uh-huh. I can see that. How do you suppose that happened?"

Aaron looked everywhere but at his father while he thought about that. He then pulled himself up onto his knees and ran a pudgy finger through the dirt in the vacant habitat. "I fink Caroline did it. Her don't like him."

Mike frowned. What Aaron meant was he didn't like her. The wedding was less than two months away. And getting closer every day. "No, she didn't like him too much, huh? Maybe that was because of the way you surprised her by sticking him in her face when she was over here Sunday. But I don't think she let him out, Aaron. And neither do you."

His bottom lip poked out stubbornly. "I don't want Caroline no more. I just like you an' my Julie an' my froggy an' my grandma-lady."

Mike straightened up and ran his hand over his mouth. He wondered if Aaron had said any of this to Caroline. Geez. Going to sit on his son's bed, he scooped him up into his arms and held him close to his chest. The sweet baby softness of him warmed Mike's heart. He rested his chin on Aaron's head. "Come on, big guy. You used to like Caroline. Why don't you like her now?"

"'Cause her's mean. Her lells at you 'bout Julie. And Julie's my friend."

Mike pulled back a little to look down into Aaron's face. How much had he heard of their arguing? "Aaron, I'm going to marry Caroline. You know that."

Aaron poked out his bottom lip. "No. I don't want you to. I just like Julie 'cause she likes my froggy, an' she gots the grandma-lady at her house. I want her to live wif us."

In light of such dogged resistance, Mike deliberately sidetracked his son by playfully pulling at the baby fat on the boy's side. "Who? The grandma-lady? You want her to come live with us?"

Aaron stiffened in a snorting laugh. "No. She gots a daddy. But her can visit her girl here wif us."

Mike snorted out a laugh. "Is the grandma-lady paying you to say these things, or what?"

"No. I don't gots no money."

"Then, I guess you'd better get a job, boy. How about frog-watcher?" Mike pitched backward on the bed, the signal for a little male rough-housing. A few minutes later, he sat up and swatted at a giggling, collapsed Aaron with a pillow. "Hey, amigo, let's find your frog and then we'll get something to eat, okay?"

Aaron immediately sat up. "Yah! Can Julie go wif us?"

Mike's expression fell. But after thirty minutes of Aaron's cajoling and pleading, Mike caved in—against his better judgment, and found himself, with Aaron in tow, standing in front of Julie's door. Surely, she wouldn't smack him between the eyes if he had his kid with him? Hell, he was just doing this for Aaron. No reason why his son couldn't see his friend, just because his father couldn't control his testosterone. Wasn't that what she'd said last Saturday?

Julie opened her door. On this rare cold evening, she had on thick socks, pink sweatpants and a white long-john shirt. Her shoulder-length auburn curls looked like she'd been twisting them with her fingers. In her hands was a bowl of ice cream. Tucked under her arm was a paperback book. Definitely gorgeous. Especially her wide-eyed, ice blue stare.

"Hi. Just so you'll know, this is the big guy here's idea." He jerked his thumb toward Aaron. "We're here to ask you to go eat with us. Or have you already eaten?"

She held his gaze for a moment before glancing down at the bowl of melting ice cream in her hands, and then back up at him. "No. I haven't eaten. But what prompted this? I don't get it, Mike—after Monday."

Mike's gut tightened. For two cents, he'd walk away. But, hell, he was here now. Exhaling slowly, he shrugged. "No big deal. It just seems our erstwhile amphibian absconded, and we're sad."

Setting her bowl and her book down on the end table just inside her door, she looked from him to Aaron and back to him. "Your what…did what— What did you say?"

Suddenly, the whole thing was funny. Mike grinned. "I said, Kermit took a powder and is on the lam."

Clearly still at sea, she leaned toward him. "What?"

Mike huffed out another breath and tried again…slowly. "The…frog…is…gone…and…we're…sad. Some of us more than others." He nodded his head down at Aaron and raised his eyebrows at her, hoping to convince her to help him out and play along.

She came along right nicely. "Oh, I get it! The frog is gone, and you're sad!" She smiled brightly, but then her eyes widened in belated understanding. Her hands went to her mouth. Then she leaned down to comfort Aaron. "Oh, I'm so sorry, Aaron. Maybe he'll come back."

Mike couldn't seem to take his eyes off her. When he spoke, she straightened up to face him. "Well, he isn't actually gone. He's loose somewhere in our apartment."

"O-o-h, yuck."

"Spoken like a true female. But be careful here. Saying things like that can cause you to lose some serious Julie-points."

He loved how she frowned when she didn't understand something. It caused a little wrinkle right between her gorgeous eyes. "Julie-points? Do I want to know what those are?"

"You'll sleep better at night if you don't. Now, are you going to come with us weary frog pursuers to hunt down some supper, or not?" He wasn't happy with the way he was holding his breath while he waited for her reply. Worst of all, she looked like she was going to say no. He sobered. "It's only a meal, Julie. Nothing else. I swear. Just between friends, okay?"

Even though he didn't really feel like it, he smiled hugely in encouragement. She locked gazes with him. Every reason why she shouldn't go, and why he shouldn't be here, was reflected in her eyes. But then she turned again to Aaron.

"Do you want me to come with you, Aaron?"

"Yeah. I asked my daddy if you could. And he said okay."

She grinned at the boy, ruffled his hair and straightened up. Mike watched her every move and wondered to himself, for about the tenth time, just what the hell he thought he was doing here. But he managed an answering grin when she gestured broadly and announced, "Then, hunting down supper, it is."

Thirty minutes later, allowing Julie time to make herself presentable, which turned out to mean throwing on a pair of jeans and a sweater, Mike didn't hunt any farther than the Pepper's around the corner from their apartments. He got out of his Blazer, and then, trotting around to the passenger's side to help Julie and Aaron do the same, he joined them in enjoying the smells of the crisp night air, heavy with the beef-scented hickory smoke that escaped from the restaurant's grill vent. When his stomach grumbled irritably, Mike clutched at it. Julie and Aaron turned laughing faces to him.

"So, Mike, are you hungry?"

"Daddy's tummy thundered."

"Hey. It could have been worse," he assured them.

Julie held up a hand. "Please don't elaborate. I have a brother."

"Yes, ma'am." And then suddenly, Mike felt...well, dammit, giddy. It might have been unmanly—he could see Sal laughing at him already—but he was consciously and totally happy, like he hadn't been for...a long time. He wanted to jump up and give a war whoop. The night was black, starlit and blessedly cool, and he was with Julie. It couldn't last. It shouldn't even be happening. But too bad. He intended to enjoy the moment, anyway. He'd pay later—and gladly. But tonight was his.

After they were seated, Aaron next to Julie, Mike across

the table from them, he faced her in the soft half light and held her gaze. He spared Aaron a glance and grinned at the picture his son made sitting next to her. Completely content now that he'd won the mock battle over who got to sit by Julie, the little turkey was preoccupied with singing softly to himself and coloring his cartooned place mat with the crayons the waiter had given him.

"So," Mike said, looking back at Julie, "what's new with you since you threw me out of your office on Monday?"

Julie's laughter heartened him. "I did not throw you out. But, to answer your question, not much. Dan—my crazy brother you met in the men's room—and his wife, Joan, have gone home. But my sister and her family are still here. They go back to California this weekend. She says Tommy is still talking about Aaron."

"Yeah, Tommy's a good kid. They seemed to hit it off." *Like us,* he almost added.

"Good thing, since they'll soon be cousins—sort of." She looked down at her hands and fiddled with a silver ring on her right ring finger. "I guess we will be, too."

Mike thankfully didn't have to say anything to that because their waiter brought their drinks right then.

But the happiness began to drain right out of him, just like the sugar that he poured into his iced tea. *Here we go. Well, what had he expected? One thing was for certain, he'd better nail down—and fast—exactly what he was about, being here with her. Because Caroline represented the rest of his life. Then, what was Julie?*

Julie looked up at him. "Did…did Caroline stay with you while she was here?"

Mike stirred his tea and held her gaze steadily. No way was that an innocent question—or any of her business. But still, he answered. "No. She stayed in Tampa." He barely stopped himself before confessing that he hadn't slept with Caroline on this trip, and that all they'd done was fight. About her.

She nodded. "But she's gone now, right? I mean, for the time being?"

Mike watched her for a moment before answering, and wished he could read her mind. "Yeah. Earlier this evening. We took her to the airport."

"Oh. And then, as soon as she left, you came to my apartment?"

Her words slapped him across the face. He'd never thought about how it would look. "It wasn't like that, Julie. I swear."

Looking like she didn't believe him for a minute, she gave her attention to Aaron, who showed her his artwork. Mike watched her easy way with his son. The kid loved her. While she bent over Aaron, Mike had to stop himself from reaching out to brush the red curls out of her face. He wanted to see more of her. No. He had to be honest. He *needed* to see more of her.

Leaning forward in the booth, just enough to brace his elbows on the table, Mike rested his chin on his hands. *What was it about this woman that kept drawing him back to her?* As if she'd read his mind and was going to answer that for him, she looked up. Though he knew he should, Mike couldn't look away to save his life. Luckily, Aaron went happily back to his creation, but Julie sobered and bit at her bottom lip, frowning enough to make that little vertical line reappear between her eyes.

"You know, you have an intense way of looking at someone that makes them feel really uncomfortable. Or guilty."

Mike grinned. "The FBI taught me that."

"No lie. Stop it."

"Yes, ma'am." But he didn't. He couldn't.

She thunked her glass of water down on the cardboard coaster. "I really like Caroline. She'll be a good mother to Aaron."

There it was. Mike sat back, extending his arms out to

grasp the back of the booth. "I know. That's why I'm marrying her."

Sparing Aaron a glance, apparently to assure herself that he wasn't listening to them, Julie leaned forward. Her eyes looked like ice chips in the harsh light of the brass fixture that hung above their table. She kept her voice low. "Shouldn't that be just one of the reasons? I mean, there are about nine million women around who'd make him a good mother. What about you, Mike—your feelings? Don't they count for something?"

Mike ran a hand over his face. "Did you minor in psychology, Julie? Damn. Okay, so I'm guessing your point is, if I'm so in love with Caroline, then what am I doing here with you?"

She sat back. "Bingo."

Well, it wasn't like he hadn't known it was coming. "Okay. Okay. I just thought it was supper. But if it's more, then what are *you* doing here with me?"

Her mouth tightened. "I'm here for Aaron. We're friends, remember?"

He didn't believe it. And neither did she. Well, it was partially true, he supposed. At least, he hoped that neither of them was using Aaron as an excuse.

"What about us, Julie? You don't think a man and a woman can be friends?"

"Sure, I do. But not us. We can't be friends."

Mike frowned. "Why the hell not?"

"Because…it doesn't feel like friends, Mike." Bracing her elbow on the table, she ran her fingers over her forehead as if she had a headache. Then she laughed. "God, the irony of this whole thing. I have no right to be questioning you like this, do I? I hardly know you. But I swear, someone up there must really hate me."

Mike reached out and captured her hand in his. She stared at their joined hands and then met his gaze. Her expression could only be called bleak. Mike ran his thumb over the soft back of her hand, thinking how small it was compared to his. And how cold it felt. "I doubt it."

"Well, that's one vote." She watched him rubbing her hand, then took up the battle again. "When's your wedding?"

The hot flush of anger claimed him. He let go of her and struggled to keep his voice a bare notch above a hiss. "Why in the hell are you doing this, Julie? Do you want me to say I'm a bastard? Okay. I'm a bastard."

Gaining back a modicum of control when Aaron turned his wide-eyed, frowning attention on them, Mike assured him that nothing was wrong, that Daddy and Julie were just talking about...a movie they'd seen. The waiter arrived with their food at that moment. His impersonal banter as he set the plates before them was a welcome relief.

Once Aaron was occupied with dredging his fries through a blob of ketchup on his plate, Mike took up the gauntlet Julie'd thrown down. "All right. We'll do this your way. My wedding is in less than two months. My partner, Sal Pomerantz, is my best man. Aaron here is the ring bearer. And you and your family, along with five hundred other people, should be getting invitations any day now.

"The wedding itself is in Boston at a huge cathedral. It'll be the social event of the season. And Caroline's parents—who *really* approve of their only darling marrying a divorced working stiff who already has a kid—are nevertheless flying in all the guests, including my parents from Oklahoma, and are putting you up for the full four days of the celebration. It should be a helluva party. I hope you can make it. Then, for our honeymoon, we're going to Europe—all of it. For a month. Happy now?"

She sat back and put her hands in her lap. Her face was devoid of expression. "No. Are you?"

5

"I'M AN IDIOT. A complete and total idiot, Susan. But what was I supposed to do? This…this Caroline-thing is always between us. Oh, God, the man is engaged to our cousin."

Julie stopped pacing in her parents' living room and faced her sister. Susan, looking cool and comfortable in a linen maternity top and pants, sat ensconced in an over-stuffed chair. She also wore a rapturous expression as she dipped a hot pickled cauliflower into the bowl of lime sherbet that rested on her rounded abdomen. Julie made a disgusted noise. "That is so gross."

Susan looked up, appearing surprised that she wasn't alone, and then chewed hurriedly and swallowed. "What is?"

"Are you even listening to me?" Julie perched a hip on the end of the mauve leather couch across from her sister's chair and crossed her arms.

"I'm listening. But you better be careful. I think Mom's bugged the house." When Julie made a face, Susan fished another piece of the cold vegetable out of the jar and added, "Look, kiddo, take some advice from your older sister. Let him go. Keep this up and it's heartbreak city for you—and you alone."

"I know, I know." Julie stood up and paced the room, finally stopping to stare out the patio doors at the golf course. Pairs of Saturday golfers moved over the grounds like industrious ants.

She watched them a moment, before a sudden thought whipped her around. "Then why does he keep coming to me? I never go to him. He's been at my door twice—okay, the first time Mom dragged him there—but he's also come to my work. You were there. And then he showed up at my apartment on…what was it? Wednesday? Yeah, Wednesday—the same evening he took Caroline to the airport. And then, bam! He's at my door with Aaron and wanting me to go eat with them.''

Julie watched as Susan dragged her treat through the sherbet. ''How can you eat that? You're making me sick.''

Susan pooh-poohed that notion with a dismissive noise. ''You'll understand one day. But, hey, did you go with him?''

''Yes. But I picked a fight. That's why I'm an idiot.''

Susan chewed, looked thoughtful, and then wiped her chin with a napkin. ''I don't think you are. I think you're protecting your heart against the day when you're going to see those little napkins with the silver lettering up in Boston that say something like Mike Loves Caroline and the wedding date.''

Julie sat up straighter. ''Is that what I'm doing—protecting my heart?''

''Sure.'' Then she made a face. ''I think so. I don't know. Are you?''

Julie laughed and tugged at her rayon dress, straightening out the twists in it as it cascaded over her legs. ''Thanks. You're a lot of help.''

Susan grinned. ''What are big sisters for?''

Julie crossed her arms and gave a derisive snort. ''Yeah, right. If you were being a good big sister, you never would've let Mom invite Mike and Aaron here today.''

Susan managed to look guilty, but Julie didn't believe it for a minute. ''Oh, come on, Julie. I consider it a victory of sorts that Mom even asked you how you felt about them being here *before* she asked them. She must have gone through sensitivity training since I got married.

''And anyway, it's not my house. I don't issue invitations, and I don't have a say in who gets them. She says she did it for Tommy. He's been begging all week to see Aaron, and we're leaving tomorrow. We just all sort of caved in, because Mr. Tommy thinks his new chum is pretty neat-o keen. You should have been here. It was so cute. Mom called Mike and then let Tommy talk with Aaron to ask him to come today.''

"I'm sure it was precious—two three-year-olds on the telephone.''

Susan smirked. "We got to hear all about you.''

Julie's smile vanished. "What do you mean?''

"It seems, baby sister, that one young man, namely Aaron DeAngelo, is quite taken with you.''

Relieved that the name in question was Aaron, she smiled. "Yeah, he's a cute little squirt.''

"Just like his father.''

"Shut up.''

"Whatever you say. Hey, where're you going?''

Julie practically ran to the tiled foyer. "Was that a car?'' She peeked out through the lace curtains. Yes, it was a car. But it wasn't a Blazer. It drove on by, continuing down the wide road. She ignored the aching disappointment that gripped her belly as she let go of the curtain panel and turned back to the living room.

Susan called out. "You're awfully dressed up today for a barbecue, Julie. Is that a new dress?''

Rounding the corner back into the room, Julie dragged herself to the couch and flopped onto it. "Shut up. I didn't buy it because Mike will be here. I bought it because I like it.''

"And that's the story you're sticking with, right?'' She then turned a mocking expression on her sister's graceless repose. "Well, that's attractive. I sit like that because I'm nearly six months pregnant. What's your excuse?''

With her fingers interlaced over her belly, Julie just made a face at her. She then sat up attentively and twisted around at the sound of a door opening in the kitchen behind her.

She listened for a moment, hearing voices. "Mom and Tommy are back."

"She probably bought out the grocery store. Hey, ten bucks says Tommy has a new toy."

Julie snorted and turned around, only to flop back down in her original position. "No way. That's a sucker bet. Her only grandchild not get a new toy every time she leaves the house with him? Yeah, right."

"Julie? Susan? Where are you, sweeties?"

The two sweeties grinned at each other. Susan quickly put her bowl and the jar on the mahogany table to the other side of her before calling out, "We're in here, Mom." She eyed her sister. "Not a word about my snack, either. Here she comes."

"Like she can't see the evidence." Julie settled more fully into her ungainly flop.

"Here you are," Ida said as she approached them, rounding the corner of the couch to face Julie. "Look who drove up right behind me!"

Instant déjà vu. She was holding Aaron DeAngelo's hand.

"Aaron!" Julie bolted upright just as the little boy launched himself into her arms. She hugged him fiercely, even as she looked around for his father. But he was nowhere to be seen. Surely Mike hadn't just dropped Aaron off and left. Well, it wasn't important, because she had her arms full of his precious little guy. "How's my friend, sweetheart?"

"I'm okay. I came to see my 'nother friend, too— Tommy. He gots a new toy at the store. See? It's bubbles, an' he got me some."

He pulled back to show her a red plastic bottle and a wand to match. "Hey, those are pretty nifty," Julie said. "But where is Tommy?"

Ida answered. "He had to visit the bathroom. Come on, Aaron, let's go get him, and then we'll go out back and blow lots of bubbles." She took Aaron's hand and turned to her daughters. "Susan, put away that cauliflower before you make yourself sick. And then you two come on outside. It's beautiful."

With that parting comment, Ida disappeared into the dining room with Aaron. Julie raised an I-told-you-so eyebrow at her sister, who studiously ignored her at first, but then groused, "How does she do that?"

"You're asking me?" Grinning, she jumped up to help Susan lever herself out of the chair. Susan picked up her bowl and the jar, taking them into the kitchen. Julie followed her.

"So," Susan began, "do you suppose little Mr. De-Angelo did indeed drive himself here?"

Done with the dishes, Julie preceded her sister to the patio doors. She shrugged. "We're about to find out, aren't we?"

Aaron had definitely not driven himself the twenty or so miles south from Brandon to Sun City Center. Nor had he been dropped off for the afternoon. For there stood his tall, dark and handsome father by the screen-covered pool. Julie's heart dropped at the sight of him, one hand in his jeans pocket, his muscular legs slightly apart, a can of beer in his other hand. He was laughing with her father and Ben as they stood close to the smoking barbecue grill. Even though he faced her, he hadn't seen her yet.

"I swear he just gets more and more gorgeous every time I see him. You poor thing."

Julie ignored her sister's whispering in her ear as she gripped her elbow. No one had to tell her how showstopping Mike DeAngelo was. Or how deserving of pity she was for caring more than she should. Her palms slickened as she clutched at her dress and wondered if he was still mad at her for her behavior on Wednesday at Pepper's.

Then he looked up and saw her. His expression changed, became…yearning? He didn't say anything, but all of a sudden, beer spurted out the top of his can and ran over his hand. He jumped back in reaction as the brew splattered his cowboy boots. While the two other men looked perplexed, he brought the newly dented can to his lips to suck up the excess.

"Damn, boy, no more beer for you," Jack Cochran teased.

Ben handed him a golf towel that he snatched off a peg attached to the house. "Here, use this. Then you can suck the beer out of it later, since the host and barkeep here cut you off."

"Ben!" Susan chastised her husband. She dragged Julie forward with her, stopping when she reached them. "That's gross."

Ben pushed a lock of blond hair off his forehead and widened his blue eyes teasingly at his wife. Putting an arm around her shoulders, he kissed her temple. "Unlike eating sherbet and cauliflower together, right?"

"That's different." Susan playfully pinched at her husband's side and turned to Mike. "Hi, Mike. We're glad you could come today. Tommy's been so excited since he talked with Aaron on Thursday."

Mike grinned. "Thanks for asking us. Aaron's been talking about this for two days straight. All I've been hearing about, since Ida called, is coming to the grandma-lady's house."

Since "Ida" called? When had her mother become Ida to him? Julie watched him with her family. He just looked so darned right, being here. It wasn't fair. She quickly reminded herself that he was engaged to her cousin. And she'd better accept it. *Yeah, right.* Still, the little reminder her angelic conscience poked at her made her frown.

Then Mike trained his attention on her, drawing her in, erasing her troubled thoughts. "You look really nice, Julie. I like you in that dress."

Was it just her, or had he managed to make his comment sound like he'd like her better *out* of the dress? Either way, she felt her face heat up as the men all stared at her appreciatively.

"It's new, and she bought it because she likes it," Susan informed him. She then turned slightly to beam at her little sister and raise an eyebrow, as if to remind her that it was her turn to speak.

Had not everyone's attention been on her, Julie would have glared at Susan. As it was, she was forced to be cordial. "Thank you, Mike. Um, you look nice, too." *Stupid, stupid, stupid—you don't tell men they look nice. See? Look at his face.* Close to a panic, Julie cast around for something not related to clothes. "Um—did you ever find your frog?"

All heads swung to him, putting the ball squarely in his court. Thank God. He addressed Julie's family first. "The frog's Aaron's. It got out of its aquarium in our apartment." He took another sip of his beer before turning back to her. "And yes, we did find him. In the toilet. But he's not the nicest person I've met recently in a bathroom."

The day heated up dangerously. Or was it just her? She returned the amused, it's-your-turn glances her family sent her way. "Well, there you have it—my claim to fame. You stumble into one wrong rest room and no one ever forgets it. Thanks for bringing it up, Mike. You're my hero."

Mike grinned, raised his presqueezed can in a salute and skewered her in place with his soft, black-eyed gaze. "I've been told that before. But the thing about heroes is, sometimes they can be real jackasses to the people they care about the most."

Into the charged silence, everyone but Mike and Julie, who were occupied with sending apology-laden goo-goo eyes at each other, began talking at once. Remarks—that the one functioning part of Julie's mind recorded—ranged from "oh, what a beautiful day," to "how about them Gators?"

Before they got back to the weather, Ida rounded a corner of the house with the two little boys in tow. Their cheerful chatter roused Julie, and apparently Mike, for he too looked their way. Julie was quite sure that Queen Elizabeth herself had never had a more effusive greeting from her subjects than Ida did from this gathering. At the burst of overly happy emotion expressed at seeing her and the boys at long last, Ida stopped short. Equally startled, Aaron and Tommy clutched at her legs.

Putting a comforting hand on each of the boys' backs, Ida frowned, opened her mouth once or twice, then pointed a thumb at the garage. "I just went to the grocery store. What's wrong with y'all?"

HERE, MIKE, THERE'S ROOM by Julie. Sit here. Something else to eat? To drink? No more beer for you, ha-ha. How's the FBI business? Julie, heard anything yet on your promotion? We're all keeping our fingers crossed! So, Mike, how go the wedding plans? Sweetie, pass that ketchup to the boys. Will Caroline be visiting again before the wedding? She's such a lovely girl. So unaffected by her wealth. Let's see, she's my mother's oldest brother's... Well, never mind. We're related somehow. Kissing cousins, I guess. Ha-ha.

And so the afternoon had gone, Julie reminisced on her way back to Brandon. Right up to where it was decided she and Mike had been silly not to have driven down together and saved the gas. He'd just looked at her, like the same idea had crossed his mind. She looked in her rearview mirror. Yep. He was still right behind her. She adjusted the rearview mirror on her BMW to reduce the glare of his headlights.

Just whose idea had it been for Aaron to stay over at her parents' house with Tommy? She thought about it. Oh, that's right—big shock—her mother's. Julie could just hear her all over again—"Oh, no big deal," the conniving little stinker had assured Mike. Aaron can sleep in a pair of Tommy's pajamas. And they'll bring him back with them tomorrow morning when they pick up Julie on their way to the airport.

And so it had been settled. And that left her and Mike alone, in their separate cars, and in a few more minutes, in their separate apartments. On a Saturday night. And it was only—she looked at the fluorescent glow of the digital clock in the dash—ten forty-five.

Just what did her mother think was going to happen? Did she think for one minute that Julie and Mike would jump each other's bones just because they had the opportunity? Julie scoffed at that thought. Who was she kidding? Her mother was positive that her baby was still a virgin since she wasn't married. No, forget that. Ida Cochran would do a lot of things, but she would not purposely set up a sexual tryst for her unmarried child.

Julie pulled into the Providence Road Apartments' parking lot. She glanced again into the rearview mirror. Mike turned right when she went left. He'd gone his way. She'd gone hers. See? She'd been silly to work herself up into giddy knots thinking that Mike might follow her to her apartment. If he had, she would have sent him packing. Well…no, she wouldn't. Oh, geez, she wanted him to pursue her. Pulling into an empty parking space, she turned off the headlights and sat there. With her hands at the top of her steering wheel, she rested her forehead on them. Forget it. Go away, lustful thoughts. No way was she going to his apartment. No way.

Way. Julie worked the clutch and slipped the gears into reverse. And stopped. Still staring straight ahead, she forced herself to analyze her thoughts, her motives, her desires. No way. She popped the gearshift into neutral and killed the engine. No way. She set the emergency brake. With conscious, resolute intention, she gathered up her purse and her sweater and got out, locking her car. Satisfied with her lofty morals, she put her keys in her purse, pulled her sweater around her shoulders, and began the walk back to Mike's apartment.

Sticking to the middle of the lit parking lot, Julie strode on purposefully, all the while listening to the night sounds around her. There was always the traffic, the cars whizzing by on Providence. But, somehow, the motorized noises mixed amicably with the frogs croaking, the owls hooting and a subdued conversation that was coming from a tiny patio she passed. She walked on, keeping the tennis courts to her right, the buildings to her left, and her thoughts on anything but what she was actually doing.

Just as she congratulated herself on so successfully immersing her psyche in denial, she very nearly screamed out loud when she rounded a corner and ran smack into a large, solid someone who grabbed her arms. Shadowed by the overhanging branches of a two-hundred-year-old, moss-draped oak, which hid the winter moon's pale light, Julie could not clearly see her...what? Attacker? Accoster? Poor slob out for a walk, just like her?

Praying for the third scenario, she mumbled "excuse me" at the same time Mike did. *Mike did?* Julie froze for a numbing second. The implications were too horrible, too wonderful. "Mike! Is that you?"

"Julie?"

"Mike! It is you!"

"Julie! What are you doing out here?"

Well, now. How to answer that question. Stalling, she looked everywhere but at him as he turned her into the moonlight. "I'm, um... What am I doing out here? The same thing you are."

Silence. "You were bringing me a picture Aaron drew for me at his baby-sitter's?"

That was the best he could come up with? Pathetic. But it was better than her excuse. "No, of course not, silly. I was, um, bringing you a brochure on my bank's new...checking account services. In case you might want to...switch...to my bank." *Lame. World-class lame.*

"At quarter to eleven at night on a Saturday?"

"We have extended hours, too."

"I guess you do." He had the nerve to laugh at her story. "So, where's this brochure?"

Brochure? "Where's the picture Aaron drew?"

Damned if he didn't hand her one. She held it up to the light. "You wanna give me a hint here?"

"It's you."

She moved it closer to her face. No. Maybe it was upside down. She turned it around. "Ah. There we are. Hey, a remarkable likeness. I see he studied under Picasso."

"Yeah, I kinda thought the same thing. Especially since both of your eyes are on the same side of your head."

"Strangely enough, that's not the first time I've been told that."

And suddenly, the whole situation seemed incredibly, stupidly funny. Hilariously funny. Sitting-on-the-curb, holding-your-sides funny.

When she could talk, Julie rubbed at her watering eyes and said the first thing that came to mind. "You do realize, of course, that we are absolutely pathetic?"

"Hey, we passed pathetic with that picture and bank brochure thing."

Julie hit him. "Don't tell me you drew this picture yourself."

"Seriously, Aaron drew it. And he's right proud of it, ma'am."

Julie looked at it again. "Well, then, I'm appropriately flattered, and I'll thank him and hang it on my refrigerator." She smiled again at the loving crayon tribute to her. But then she smelled a rat. Frowning at him in a sidelong glance, she accused, "Why didn't you just bring it with you to Mom's today?"

He pulled back and looked at her. "What? And miss this Kodak moment?"

Julie laughed with him, but refused to be sidetracked. "You'd better tell me you didn't know beforehand that Aaron was going to stay over."

He crossed his heart. "Swear to God, I did not."

Julie grinned. He looked just like a sincere little boy. Except he was this devastatingly handsome and sexy man. "All right, I believe you. And, Mike, I owe you an apology for last Wednesday. I mean, here you were being a nice guy and asking me to dinner, and I acted like this big jerk—"

"Forget it, Julie. It's no big deal. And, hell, I wasn't just being nice. I wanted to see you as much as Aaron did. Speaking of that little turkey, he says you're his girlfriend now." Mike stared right into her eyes. "He really likes you, you know. I mean—a lot."

Julie smiled, feeling all warm inside. "Aaron is special to me, too. Just like his daddy."

Then the moment stretched out, got serious. Mike reached over and took her hand in his. Looking into her eyes, he asked, "So, what do we do now?"

Julie could barely breathe, much less make a rational decision. His touch was so...*welcome.* That was the best word she could come up with. Whenever he touched her, it just felt so darned right. What was she going to do? Well, she'd come this far. No sense chickening out now. Like Tennyson always said, "'Twas better to have loved and lost, than never to have loved at all." 'Twas also better not to think at all at this point. "Well, the way I see it, we decide on your place or mine."

His eyebrows shot up. "Yeah? I vote for both."

He was teasing. She knew that. But still, there it was. This thing between them. They were right on the edge. Was it just a matter of one hormone calling to another? She looked over at him. How was it possible that he was even better-looking in the moonlight? No, what she felt for him was so far beyond simple lust that it scared her. Given that, could she allow it to be dragged through the dirt? Well, she had warned herself not to think. Her mood slumped right along with her shoulders. "We can't do this, Mike, can we?"

"No, we can't." He said it quickly enough, but then he frowned. "Why can't we?"

Julie bit back a grin. There it was again—that little boy look of his. "Because you and I...we're not just us."

Mike looked off toward the tennis courts and nodded. He sat with his knees bent and spread apart, his elbows atop them, with his hands folded in between them. He finally brought his attention back to her, resting his chin on his biceps. His eyes were glossier than the night. Points of moonlight danced in them, giving off silver reflections. "I sure don't have any answers for you, Julie. Hell, I don't even know the questions. All I know is I'm not playing, and I want to kiss you again. But all over, this time."

Julie sucked in a ragged breath. "Mike, don't say things like—"

"And then do it again…slower."

"Please. You're—"

"What I am is on fire for you."

Oh, God, he was pursuing her, just like she'd wanted him to, not more than five minutes ago. He hadn't moved a muscle toward her, but already her body was opening up for him, making ready to receive him. One or two more words from him, and she'd slide right off the curb into the gutter. For real.

And yet he still didn't move a muscle. He just held her gaze. There were fifty reasons why they shouldn't do this. And only one overpowering reason why they should. As if to second this, an arc of sexuality sparked from him to her and back again. Julie realized that her mouth was open and that she was breathing in half measures. Panting. She was panting for him.

Mike stood up with one graceful, athletic move and held his hand out to her. "Julie, I can't walk away from you tonight on my own. Either tell me to go away, or come with me now. It's your decision."

Julie stared at his hand. She wanted him. She'd already told herself that she loved him. Now was the time to find out. Her hand clutched almost involuntarily into a fist at her side. What about Caroline? *Well, he didn't look too concerned with his fiancée. Why should you be?*

Why, indeed. Then, right or wrong, it was settled. She

was going to do this. Slowly, after two half starts and after she laid aside her sweater, purse and Aaron's picture, she finally put her hand out and grasped his. Lightning should have rent the night when she touched him. Thunder should have boomed overhead. The heavens should have split. But none of that happened.

Except inside her. Mike pulled her to her feet and into his arms. He was kissing her, and it was all that mattered. Until they heard the friendly hooting and encouraging catcalls of their neighbors on their balconies. Mike pulled back from her, grinned down into her face, and then turned slightly to hold her hand up with his in a victory salute to their audience. Applause broke out.

Julie wanted to hide under a bush, but Mike still had a firm grip on her. Grinning hugely, he looked back down at her. "This is a little too public for me."

"I'll say." Not a brilliant comment, but it was all she could manage with no air in her lungs and Mike's kiss still wet on her lips. Sucking in a few gulps of air, she added, "Let's go to my place. I don't think I could—I mean, Aaron's stuff is there, and Caro—"

"Stop right there—please." He stopped rubbing his hands up and down her arms to grip her tightly. "Tonight, just think about us. We'll go to your place. But I still have to go to my apartment first."

Julie frowned at him.

Mike rubbed a hand over his mouth. His expression could only be dubbed self-conscious. "Um, okay—straight out. I have to get a condom. Or two. I'm not like a lot of guys who carry them in their wallets, thinking they might get lucky at work or at the grocery store."

Had he not been holding on to her with one hand, Julie would have walked off into the overgrown vegetation at the back of the complex and kept on going until she died from embarrassment. *Say something. You're a woman of the nineties.* "Well, I guess I should be glad, huh? I mean, that proves you weren't so sure of...the outcome. Or of me. Or of yourself. Or—" *Okay, that was good. Now, shut up.*

Mike made an I-see-your-point face, and then grinned, probably thinking he'd come off looking pretty good. "Yeah. I mean, no, I wasn't. Oh, hell, I never have been able to convince myself to carry the damn things around with me. Guys like that—well, you know."

Maybe. "Do you want me to just go on to my—" she indicated the direction of her apartment "—or should I go with…?"

His hesitation vanished. "You're going with me."

He said it so adamantly that Julie had to laugh. "Afraid I'll change my mind and lock you out?"

"Yes. And I don't want to be the subject of tomorrow's headlines because I had to break down your door to ravish you. Wouldn't the bureau love that?"

"Ravish me? Would you?"

"In an Oklahoma minute, sweetheart," Mike assured her, managing to look a little satyrlike. He picked up the picture, her purse and sweater, and handed them to her.

Julie clutched them tightly. A tittering thrill of sexual awareness swept over her. "Oklahoma minutes? Are those any different from Florida minutes?"

He pretended to think about that as he took her elbow and started walking toward his apartment. "Maybe. But those Oklahoma minutes can have you roped, tied and branded before you can blink."

"Well. When you put it that way, it sounds like fun."

"You're about to find out just how much fun, baby."

6

JULIE STARED UP at the ceiling in her bedroom, but she wasn't seeing. Instead, she saw trumpeting angels and harp-playing cherubs. She saw scudding clouds and windswept cliffs, thundering herds of powerful horses, a Roman orgy. And all because Mike DeAngelo had touched her body. Oh, God, had he touched her body. She was a changed woman. It was all she could do not to jump up in bed, naked as a Thanksgiving Day turkey, and belt out a chorus from the musical *Oklahoma! Oh, baby, let those winds sweep on down the plains.*

She returned to earth when Mike shifted his sweat-slickened weight. Breathing a little more normally now, he lay on his stomach with an arm and a leg draped posses-sively over her. He raised his head up to give her a look hot enough to scorch the wallpaper. Then, with purely sen-sual calculation on his face, he bent and captured her nip-ple. Julie arched in moaning encouragement, clutching des-perately at his thick hair as he mercilessly swirled and sucked at the already swollen and tender peak.

She nearly passed out before he took pity on her and quit, but only so he could pull himself up over her more fully and capture her lips. A jolt of desire rocked her. His mouth tasted of her own musk. Completely surrendered, Julie flung her arms around his neck and gave him full access to plunder her mouth. Oh, what that mouth of his could do. Her nipples weren't the only parts of her that were swollen and tender. As if naming themselves, her hips bucked against him with a will of their own.

Mike broke their kiss. Julie opened her eyes. His passion-darkened face wasn't more than three intimate inches from her own as he supported himself on his elbows. He held her pinned under him while he reached out with his fingertip and ran it over her face with wonder, as if he were a blind man using his sense of touch to see her. Julie could barely breathe as she in turn memorized his handsome, chiseled features. The moment was so magical, so fragile. What did he see when he looked at her?

He cupped her chin, forcing her to look into his eyes. "I want to love you until you make that little sound at the back of your throat again, Julie." He bent his head to kiss her earlobe, her jaw, her neck.

Julie sucked in a ragged breath. "I'd die if you didn't."

Mike raised his head and smiled. A smile that told of pleasures to come. "Well, now, we wouldn't want that. Good thing I picked up a handful of condoms at my apartment, instead of just two, huh?"

Julie pinched his arm. Or tried to. Rock-hard muscle just wasn't pinchable. "A handful? Piggy."

He chuckled, just enough to shake the bed, and her with it. "Piggy? Damn. And here I thought I was the big, bad wolf."

Julie grinned right back at him. "Be real careful right here, buddy. If you're the wolf, does that make me a pig?"

He studied a point just above her head and pretended to think about that. For some reason, a slow grinding of his hips against hers seemed to help his efforts. He looked back down at her, leering intently enough to earn himself instant membership in the Lecherous Wolf Society. He reached out to capture a thick lock of her hair and tug the red curl into her line of vision. "No, ma'am. You're Little Red Riding Hood, of course."

Julie nodded slowly. "Oh, you're good. That was good."

"You've already told me that. You don't want all your nice words to go to my...head, now, do you?"

Julie wrenched her arm free so she could shove at his shoulder. "Oh, DeAngelo, that was cheap."

"Hey, you get what you pay for. You through talking yet?"

She raised her head and nipped at his chin. "Through talking."

"Well, yee-haw." With that, he rolled them both over until Julie was lying atop him. "I am all yours, ma'am. Be gentle."

Julie sat up, straddling his hips and squirming sensually until her softness snuggled firmly over his hardness. Bracing her hands on the warm granite wall of his chest, she leered down at him. "Be gentle? Like hell I will."

He started to say something, but his words died an impassioned death as she slid down him and hunched forward enough to cover his nipple with her mouth. The strangled gasps coming from him fueled Julie's efforts to please them both. Swirling her tongue and nipping at his skin, never letting her mouth lose contact with him, she worked her way over his chest, his collarbones, up the column of his neck, and then down the thinning line of black hair that bisected his rigid, muscular belly. Her nails raked over his skin, reveling in the feel of him everywhere her lips weren't.

Never before had she been so bold. The man was magnificent, just as she'd known he would be. Just as she'd feared he would be. How would she ever let him go after tonight?

When she slid down lower on him and took him in her hands, Mike jerked spasmodically and dragged her back up the length of him. "No, not again. Don't even think it. We may need it later."

Julie laughed out loud. "Can't take it, huh?"

Mike tried—and failed—to look properly macho. "No, I can't. Not after that last time. I can't control—well, you know. You were here."

Julie chuckled softly, feeling warm, loving and maybe

even a little heartbroken. "Yes, and I'm here now, too, Mike. And I need you. God, how I need you."

He reached up to stroke her face. "Julie."

She grasped at his hand, bringing his fingertips to her mouth, kissing each one in turn. His hands were so strong, so capable. She cupped his palm to her face and closed her eyes, afraid she was going to cry.

Mike stilled under her and then pulled his hand loose. Julie opened her eyes. Mike trailed his hand down her neck, across her shoulder, down her arm, stopping at her hip. "Come here, honey."

With that, he pulled her to him and rolled them over, covering her from chest to toes with his hard body. With tender kisses he outlined her face. With caressing hands, he fired her desire. With softly murmured words, he sealed her love for him. And then he slid down the passion-slickened length of her until he could take her in his mouth. Julie arched and groaned, grabbing behind her for the brass rungs of her headboard. No other man had ever touched her there before. And never would she want another man to hold her in his hands this way. Only Mike.

Desire peaked, rocking her and rippling her, like a kite tail in the wind. Rhythmic contractions rippled out from her center, tingling every nerve ending. And still Mike loved her. Head flung back, knees bent, toes dug into the sheets, her hands now clutching at Mike's thick hair, she lay suspended in time. Satiation robbed her of all but the present moment. She didn't even open her eyes when she felt Mike pull himself up and away from her. After a moment marked by the tearing of a cellophane wrapper, he came back to her and stroked her heated body. Needing him desperately, Julie clutched him to her, forcing him over her. As if he were a lifeline, she flung her arms and legs around him and clung to him as, with one slick, deft movement, he sheathed himself in her.

Julie heard her own guttural cry of carnal pleasure. Mike answered with soft words of desire, harsh words of need, low rasps of labored breathing as he rocked his hips against hers in the most primal of all acts between a man and a woman. Julie met him thrust for thrust, greedily seeking her own pleasure, even as she gave back to him in equal measure. When Mike's tempo increased, when his thrusts threatened to tear her asunder, when he swelled to fill her more completely, Julie feverishly raked at his muscled back, feeling her own need ready to burst yet again. And when it came for them, the moment tilted on its axis, taking her over the edge with Mike, completely content to fall in his arms, no matter the depth.

Mike collapsed heavily on her. She held him to her, accepted his weight, rubbed her hand up and down his back. With his head on her pillow, his breath came hot and labored on her cheek. Julie closed her eyes and smiled. Never in her life had she ever been this happy, this content. This…loving between them was so right. For her, he made the world fade away. He lit up the night with his smile. His laugh sent goose bumps romping over her skin. How could she ever let him go? She hugged him to her tightly and kissed his glistening forehead.

"Not…again. I swear…you'll…kill me." Mike sounded like he was begging for his life. Or for oxygen.

Julie chuckled. "Oh, please? Just once more?"

Mike pulled up on an elbow and looked down at her. Eyes narrowed, he snatched up a pillow and playfully bopped her with it. Julie giggled, which turned into a screech when he yanked her to him with a growl and turned her back to his chest. She settled immediately when he put a muscled, tanned arm around her torso and held her to him, like two nestling spoons in a silverware case. "Be still, Red Riding Hood. We have to rest now. No one makes love all night long. That's a myth men put out to make themselves look good."

Julie grinned. "I suspected as much."

"Um-hmm, I'm sure you did. Now, let me hold you for a while, and then I have to go. Before I fall asleep."

Would it be so awful if you stayed over? Julie frowned, feeling cheap, somehow. But still she pulled Mike's arm more securely around her and nestled against him. She closed her eyes, squeezing them shut, as if doing so could keep the truth of their lives away.

JULIE JERKED TO INSTANT wakefulness. *What? Who?*

She heard it again. Someone was knocking on the door. Good Lord, what time was it? She glanced at the clock on her nightstand, rubbed her still sleepy eyes and looked again. Nine-twenty. *Please.* She flopped back over on her back and lay there, staring up at the ceiling. Nine-twenty? Oh, geez, her parents were supposed to be here at…oh, God, nine-fifteen. This was awful. *Okay, Julie, get up and answer the door. Start there.*

She ripped back the sheet that covered her and jumped out of bed. Catching her reflection in her dresser's mirror, she asked herself why she was naked. She never slept naked. Then, sudden remembrance assailed her. Oh, criminy—Mike! Where was Mike? Almost fearfully, she looked again at her bed. Gone. Empty. She put a hand to her fluttering heart. Last night she'd been upset at the prospect of him doing a wham-bam-thank-you-ma'am routine and leaving, but now she was eternally grateful for his good instincts.

Until he opened the bathroom door, wearing only a towel. Julie stifled a scream by clamping her hands over her mouth. Mike stared at her. "Tell me that wasn't a knock I just heard at your door."

She moved her hands a bare inch. "I wish to God I could." Suddenly remembering her state, she grabbed at the bedsheet, tugging it desperately, until she'd pulled enough of it loose to cover her. "What are we going to do? Do you know who that is?"

"My money and my prayers are on the paperboy."

Julie nearly screeched. "It's not the paperboy, Mike. It's

not the paperboy at all. It's your worst nightmare. That's who it is. Your worst nightmare."

He didn't even hesitate. "Your mother? What in the hell is your mother doing here?"

"Oh, she's not alone. My whole family is with her. We're all going to brunch and then to the airport with Susan and Ben, remember?"

Mike just looked at her. "What are we going to do?"

In her agitation, Julie clutched at her sheet with one hand and danced in place. She waved her other hand as if trying to dry nail polish. "I asked you first. Help me!"

The knocking sounded again. Julie heard her mother calling out, "Julie, honey!"

The dancing and hand-waving intensified, despite her best effort to remain calm.

Federal Agent Mike DeAngelo went into action. Pacing and gesturing, resembling a scantily clad professor making a particularly important point, he outlined their plan. "Okay. Okay."

"Hurry!"

"I am. Okay. First we've got to pick up all my clothes." Not waiting for him, Julie dropped her sheet and raced naked around the room gathering them up. She shoved them in his arms. "Good. Okay, now, where're my boots?" She knelt by the bed, bottom up in the air, and dug his boots out from the tangled covers on the floor and flung them at him. He caught them deftly. She stood up, hands to her waist, breathing hard and awaiting more orders. He sorted through his stuff. "Okay, that's all. Now, go let them in, and I'll stay in the bathroom. Then you come back here—by yourself—and get dressed. Once you've all cleared out, I'll leave. How's that sound?"

The knocking on the door intensified. Julie stared at Mike. There was something wrong with his plan, but she couldn't put her finger on it. Mike looked her up and down and then tugged his towel off and flung it to her. Okay, that was another thing she hadn't thought of.

"Wrap that around you. Tell them you were in the shower. Come on, Julie, move!"

Mike retreated to the tiny bathroom and quietly closed the door. *Oh God, oh God, oh God* was Julie's mantra as she took heavy steps into the front hallway. Despite her shaking fingers, she managed to undo the safety latch and open the door. *Yep, there they were. Mom, Dad, Ben, Susan, Tommy and, oh God oh God—Aaron!* That was what was wrong with Mike's plan! Aaron! What were they going to do with him when Mike was nowhere to be found? Maybe they hadn't gone to his apartment yet—

"Well, sweetheart, it's about time," Ida fussed as she pushed by Julie. The rest of the family trooped in behind her, eyeing Julie dubiously as they all stood around expectantly, staring at her. Except Ben. Looking somewhat embarrassed as he passed her, he took the boys with him to go look out the sliding glass doors at the parking lot.

Julie glanced back at her mother. "I was in the shower." Was that guilty voice hers?

Susan made a noise. "We can see that. So, go get dressed. We'd like to have enough time to devour the brunch at Surfers, if you don't mind. Why are you running late?"

Why, indeed. "Because…my alarm didn't go off."

"Did you even set it?"

Julie was beginning to hate Susan. "Of course I set it. What do you think I am?"

Ida stepped in. "Now, girls, this isn't getting us on the road. Julie, before you go put on your makeup, let me take Aaron to the washroom."

Julie nearly choked. "No. You can't."

Ida, already two steps into her mission, stopped and turned around. "Why not? He's had to go since we left home."

Oh God, oh God. "The toilet's broken." *Geez, right up Dad's alley.*

"Oh, it's probably nothing. I'll take a look at it," her father said.

"No! It's not the toilet at all. It's…the light. The light's out in there."

Now even Ben turned around. "You took a shower in the dark?"

Julie's mind raced. "No. It just went out a few minutes ago. And I don't have any more bulbs—so you can't change it, Dad."

Susan, the closest one in the room to Julie, waddled over to her, took her arm and spoke in a low voice. "Why are you acting so weird? What's going on?"

Julie decided to come clean. She mouthed, "Help me."

Susan frowned and mouthed, "What?"

Julie again mouthed, "Help me," and then added, "Mike's here. Mike."

Susan's eyes widened as the color drained from her face. She let go of Julie's arm and stepped back. "Oh, dear God." She turned immediately to their family. "Um, Mom, let's all take the boys down to Aaron's apartment. Maybe Mike's home by now."

Julie clutched at her sister's arm. Did Susan not understand what she'd…mouthed? Susan brushed her hand away and spoke unnaturally loud. "He may not be there yet, but I'm sure he'll be back soon. I bet he'd gone to get doughnuts or something when we called. Why don't we all go there now and wait for him?"

Getting her ploy, Julie slumped. Until Ben exchanged a look with Jack Cochran and took a step closer to his wife. "Are you okay, Susan? Your voice sounds funny."

"Of course I'm okay. Never better. Now, come on. Let's go, dammit." She was practically shrieking by now. "Humor me. I'm pregnant."

"Okay," Ben intoned, sounding very placating. "We'll all go to Mike's apartment again." Then he added grumpily. "Although, I, for one, don't see how he could've gone for doughnuts or anything else since his Blazer's in the parking lot.''

Julie stepped up beside her sister in time to see her face turn red, just before she exploded. ''You ever heard of walking to a store for exercise? People can't walk in Florida?''

Silence reigned. Then everyone began talking at once. And moving toward the door. Susan jerked it open and ushered them all out. Except for their father. ''Dad?''

''I'll wait here. I don't feel like walking for exercise or doughnuts.'' He picked up a women's magazine on Julie's coffee table and sat down on the overstuffed couch. He began flipping through the pages.

Out in the breezeway now, Susan could do nothing but gesture wildly and mouth unintelligible directions to Julie. Giving up, Julie gestured for her to go on, indicating she should stall everyone for as long as she could. Susan flung her hands out and shrugged her shoulders. Julie closed the door and faced her father.

He smiled over at her. ''You sure you don't want me to look at that toilet? Or check your utility closet for a bulb, honey?''

Julie clutched at the towel tucked in at her bosom. ''I'm sure, Dad. You just sit right there and, for God's sake, *don't move*. I mean, don't trouble yourself. And I'll go get dressed.''

''Okay. If you're sure. But first thing tomorrow, you call the office here and get the repair people over. That's their job, you know.''

Julie fled down the hall, calling back over her shoulder, ''I will, Dad. I promise.'' In her bedroom, she closed the door none too gently and pushed in the lock button on the knob. Then, standing in the middle of the room, hands knotted over her heart, she swallowed hard several times, trying to force the lump out of her throat. Never again, she promised herself.

Okay—Mike. Going to the closed bathroom door, she

opened and peeked inside. One glance revealed it was empty. Except for the toilet, sink and bathtub, of course. She whispered, "Mike?"

The shower curtain whizzed open. Julie had to stifle a screech. Mike stood there, serious, fully dressed, hands on his waist, looking like some avenging god. Who just happened to rule his domain from behind a flower-patterned shower curtain. "Are they gone?"

At least he'd whispered. "For the moment. Except my dad. He's in there reading *Cosmo*—what are the odds? The rest of them went to your apartment."

He raised his eyebrows. "Well, that's perfect, isn't it? I bet I'm not there. Why did you send them to my apartment?"

"I didn't," Julie whispered sharply. "Susan did."

"Susan did? Because…?"

"Because your son is with them, Mr. FBI Agent with the Brilliant Plan."

Mike stared at her, suddenly struck mute. He stepped out of the tub. Julie backed up to the vanity in the tiny room. Mike sat on the tub's rim and rested his hands on his knees. He looked up at her. "Have you ever noticed how all the big moments in our relationship seem to revolve around bathrooms?"

Julie could only blink at him. He was right. And he was also still in her apartment. "You've got to go, Mike. They think you went for a walk to get doughnuts."

He frowned, looking slightly addled. "What? Why would I do that? Why would I walk for exercise, only to go get doughnuts?"

Julie put her hands to her face and then to his. *Yep. His was as hot as hers.* "Look at me, Mike. You'd have to be a woman to understand that one. But what we need to concentrate on is getting you out of here—undetected. Are you with me?" She waited for him to nod. "Good. You can slip out the sliding glass doors here in my bedroom, okay? And then hurry to your apartment. Tell them there weren't any doughnuts or juice, or whatever. You'll think of something. You got all that?''

Blessedly, his eyes cleared. He stood up, pinning Julie between him and the vanity. ''Yep. I got it. One problem.''

Julie slumped. ''What?''

''Why am I dressed in the same clothes I had on yesterday?''

Julie stared at him, at his individual features, while she thought. ''Because…you're a guy and you're a slob.''

''I am not a slob.''

''You are for today. Now, go!'' She shoved him, but succeeded only in almost toppling herself into the sink behind her. When would she learn that he was as immovable as a mountain?

Mike grabbed her for a quick kiss, looked down into her eyes and said, ''One day, we're going to laugh about this.''

''Maybe when we're ninety-five. Not a day before. Now, get out of here.''

MIKE DIDN'T WAIT UNTIL he was ninety-five to find the humor in the situation. It was barely ten hours later, and here he was vegged out in his recliner, killing himself laughing. Especially when he thought about Julie's bare but sweet little butt poked up in the air as she searched under her bed for his boots. Son of a gun, she was funny! And so damned warm and loving—in bed, as well as out of it.

Shaking his head for about the fiftieth time since he'd hightailed it back to his apartment to spout that stupid walking-for-doughnuts story to her family, he realized he was finding it increasingly difficult to remember what his life was like before he'd met Julie Cochran. And that probably wasn't good. The day when he'd have to fish or cut bait was quickly approaching.

Not able to concentrate on the TV show he'd been ignoring, he clicked it off with the remote and wrestled his chair back to its upright position. Pushing himself out of its comfort, he figured he'd better check on Aaron. The big

guy was way too quiet in his room. Which probably didn't
bode well for Popeye, his frog.

But just as he started toward the hallway, someone
knocked on the front door. Jumping at the sound, Mike half
turned around. Hell, no wonder he jumped. The last time
he'd heard a knock on the door, he'd been naked in Julie's
bathroom. Anyway, whoever it was knocked like a girl.
Probably Julie. He smiled, ignoring the effect that thought
had on his...blood pressure.

Just then, a screeched "Come back!" coming from behind him, made him turn the other way. There stood Aaron
in the hallway, naked as a jaybird. On the other hand, Popeye the frog was clad in a tiny action figure getup and was
hopping madly, desperately down the hall toward Mike's
room.

"Aaron, what the—" The repeated knocking caught his
attention again. Aaron darted around him, obviously intent
on playing naked butler. Mike grabbed for him, nearly losing his balance. Too late. He should have seen that one
coming. "Aaron, don't you dare, you little pip-squeak."

Aaron ripped open the door...maybe three or four inches.
Thank you, safety latch. A couple yards from the door, and
unable to see who it was, Mike grinned. *Teach you, big
guy.* But then, Aaron stilled, as if mesmerized, and turned
his black, wide-eyed gaze on his father. Frowning at the
implications of that look, Mike went for the door.

Aaron startled him by squealing as he poked his nose,
and probably other exposed parts of himself, out through
the crack. "Open the door, Daddy! Open the door! Hurry!
Her's back!"

Her's—she's back? He could only mean Julie. Mike
called out, "Hang on, Julie. Let me get the chain un-
latched." At the same time, he pulled Aaron back and
closed the door. "You march right back into your room,
soldier, and don't you come out until you're in full-dress
uniform."

Aaron poked his bottom lip out and jumped up and down

in place. "No. I want to see her now. I don't want my clothes."

This "no" stage of Aaron's was making an old man out of him, Mike decided. He called out again through the closed door. "Hold on another sec, Julie. We have a tactical problem here." Hearing a feminine, muffled "all right," he turned his serious-father face on his son. "Let me put it this way, buddy. No clothes, no company. Now, I don't think you really want Julie to see your bare butt, do you?"

Aaron's expression went from defiant to confused to pleading. "No! Not her, Daddy. Not Julie. Mommy. Mommy's outside. Her can see my bare butt, huh?"

7

MIKE WATCHED from the doorway to Aaron's room as Victoria sat on their son's bed, getting reacquainted. He kept his gaze on the now-dressed Aaron, hoping to figure out what this sudden visit from his mother might do to the kid's head. Not to mention his little heart. Aaron looked...what? Shy? Like he was holding back, somehow, even as he identified for her the treasures he'd laid out for her inspection.

But Mike wasn't surprised. Victoria, to Aaron, wasn't much more than postcards and presents and telephone calls from far away. Still, he couldn't help but compare how Aaron acted when he was with Julie, to how he was acting now with his own mother. Night and day. With Julie, Aaron was his completely quirky, little stinker, three-year-old self, always laughing and hugging her. He did none of those things with Tory. Or Caroline, come to think of it. Interesting.

"Tory," Mike suddenly called out. She looked up at him. He shifted his weight as he leaned against the doorjamb. "You're through goat-roping in Guatemala, I take it?"

"Oh, that's cute. I was hang-gliding in Holland. And, as you can see, I didn't fall to my death. I know you're disappointed." With that, Tory turned back to Aaron. "Here, baby, put your little things away while I go get your presents. I brought you some really neat stuff from Holland. Do you know where that is?"

Aaron shook his head as he solemnly picked up his prized treasures that his mother had barely looked at.

Watching still, Mike forced himself to concentrate on his breathing. Maybe that would relax his stomach muscles. No. They constricted tighter when Tory swept by him in an impersonal cloud of very expensive but overpowering perfume. Mike struggled not to wrinkle his nose in distaste. He then winked at Aaron and turned to follow Tory outside, completely unmoved by her slender, elegant form.

Of course, a rented Jaguar. Mike knew before she ever stopped at it that the maroon status symbol was hers. Always first-class, always me-first. Tory went to the rear of the car and opened the trunk. She reached in and began handing Mike package after package. When she spoke, her voice held a hint of coolness. "You didn't notify me of your move here, Mike. That made you pretty hard to find. Was that your intention?"

Mike narrowed his eyes at his ex-wife. "All I did was move across town. If I didn't want to be found, Tory, you wouldn't find me."

"Oh, that's right. Government agent and all that."

Mike frowned. No way in hell was he going to let her get to him. He eyed her critically. She hadn't changed much from a year ago, the last time she'd shown up. Chestnut hair that fell to her shoulders in soft waves, green eyes, perfect figure, perfect skin, perfect clothes. Suddenly, he couldn't keep quiet any longer. "What are you doing here, Tory?"

She gave him a look that clearly said she found him lacking in social graces. "My, that was abrupt."

"So answer me."

She crossed her slender arms under her cashmere-covered bosom. "I already told you. I came to see my son."

"Your son?"

Tory leaned toward him and put a cool hand on his arm. "Relax. This is a short visit, nothing more. I do have something I want to talk over with you while I'm here, but it's not horrible. For now, I'm simply between assignments, and I want to see my son. Please, Mike. It's been a year."

Her hand on his arm, as much as her words, chilled him. She could plead, and she could reassure, but he knew her better. The only thing she could want to talk to him about was Aaron. FBI training helped him keep the shard of fear that ripped through him off his face and out of his voice. "You don't have to beg. I've never tried to keep Aaron away from you. But when are you leaving?"

She laughed, a high-class purring sound. "But I just got here. You hate me, don't you, Mike."

"No. That'd take too much energy. But I don't trust you."

Her smile faltering, she stepped back and gave her attention to retrieving the few remaining packages from the car's trunk. "Oh? Do you trust Julie?"

Mike nearly dropped the packages he held. "How do you—? Who told you about Julie?"

She shifted the presents to one arm and closed the trunk. Her green eyes reflected a sly gleam. "You did, of course. When I was at the door. You called out for Julie to hold on a minute—twice. Does Caroline know about Julie?"

For the first time since he'd met Julie, he was glad she was related to Caroline. Their shared bloodlines made a very long story short—at least, in this instance. "Julie is Caroline's cousin, so yeah, I guess she does know her."

"Ah, I see. How convenient."

Mike pulled himself up sharply. "What the hell does that mean?"

Tory smiled. Like the Cheshire cat. "Now, Mike, don't forget to whom you're talking. I know how your voice sounds when you speak to the woman you love."

JULIE BOPPED, lighthearted as all get out, around the corner of Mike's building—and stopped dead. Mike was standing in a pool of light by a maroon Jaguar, not twenty yards away. His back was to her. Facing her, though, was a gor-

How to validate your
Editor's FREE GIFT "Thank You"

1. Peel off gift seal from front cover. Place it in space provided at right. This automatically entitles you to receive four free books and a lovely simulated cultured pearl necklace.

2. Send back this card and you'll get brand-new Harlequin Love & Laughter™ novels. These books have a cover price of $3.50 each, but they are yours to keep absolutely free.

3. There's no catch. You're under no obligation to buy anything. We charge nothing—ZERO—for your first shipment. And you don't have to make any minimum number of purchases—not even one!

4. The fact is thousands of readers enjoy receiving books by mail from the Harlequin Reader Service®. They like the convenience of home delivery...they like getting the best new novels BEFORE they're available in stores... and they love our discount prices!

5. We hope that after receiving your free books you'll want to remain a subscriber. But the choice is yours— to continue or cancel, any time at all! So why not take us up on our invitation, with no risk of any kind. You'll be glad you did!

6. Don't forget to detach your FREE BOOKMARK. And remember...just for validating your Editor's Free Gift Offer, we'll send you FIVE MORE gifts, *ABSOLUTELY FREE!*

GET A FREE NECKLACE...

This lovely necklace will add glamour to your most elegant outfit! Its cobra-link chain is a generous 18" long, and its lustrous simulated cultured pearl is mounted in an attractive pendant! Best of all, it's absolutely free, just for accepting our no-risk offer!

geous dark-haired woman. Both of them had their hands full of packages, and they were obviously very engaged in an intense conversation.

When the woman smiled up into Mike's face, Julie clutched tighter at the glass rim of the cooled baking pan she held. Who could the woman be? A neighbor? A friend? Maybe someone she and Caroline didn't know about?

Julie knew one thing. She didn't want Mike to see her right now. What he did with his time was none of her business. She certainly had no claim on him. The brownies—a silly idea, she decided—began to weigh her down like so much cement. For two cents, she'd heave them, pan and all, over the six-foot wooden boundary fence to her right. But she couldn't lift her arms. Or move her feet. She just stood there in the shadows, afraid she was staring like some starved orphan faced with a banquet of riches she couldn't touch.

When Mike jerked upright and raised his voice to the woman, Julie heard only two words—''Julie'' and ''convenient.'' Okay, time to disappear. Julie began backing up slowly without turning around. Once she was out of the weak illumination cast on her by the breezeway lamp, she would hotfoot it away from here.

But no more than two or three steps into her retreat, someone clutched at her legs from behind. Not daring to look Mike's way, she looked down, holding the pan away from her, and saw chubby little arms encircling her thighs. Her heart sank.

Aaron peeked around her legs, calling out, ''Daddy, Mommy, look! It's Julie!''

Mommy? Surely she hadn't heard him correctly. Still, having no choice, what with Aaron glued to her, Julie forced herself to look at Mike and…Mommy. She tried to smile, but her face muscles wouldn't cooperate. So, figuring she looked like a drugged Betty Crocker with the stupid pan of brownies in her hands, she awaited her fate.

Mike was quickly approaching her, his arms loaded with

wrapped or boxed packages. "Julie," he said when he stopped in front of her, his voice clearly reflecting his surprise. Close on his heels was…Mommy. "I wasn't expecting you."

"I know." What else could she say? Julie heard him saying something else to her, heard him tell Aaron to let her go. But she couldn't take her eyes off the gorgeous woman who stood so close to Mike and who was looking at her as if she'd discovered her stealing the silverware.

A little dachshund who'd suddenly found itself competing in a race against an Arabian mare. That was her—a weenie dog dressed in jeans and a sweatshirt and carrying brownies, against the thoroughbred's sleek, cashmere outfit and bundles of expensive-looking packages. This, she concluded, was a cruel world. *And, another thing, where did Mike get these women? Caroline wasn't rich and beautiful enough for him? Oh, lovely. Now she was on Caroline's side.*

When the moment stretched out, it was Mommy, surprisingly enough, who broke the stalemate. "Hello. I'm Victoria Lane DeAngelo. Aaron's mother. And you, obviously, are Julie."

Julie blinked. *Wait a minute. V. L. DeAngelo. Aaron's mommy was the world-famous photographer and writer?* She blinked again. *Apparently so. Lovely.* "Yes. I'm obviously Julie."

"Julie gots brownies," Aaron announced proudly, drawing their attention down to him. "I can smell them. Yum."

Everyone, including Julie, stared at the brownie pan she held. Then Mommy came to the rescue. Again. "Why don't we take all these packages inside and have one of Julie's yummy brownies? Then we can get to know each other."

"No." It was out before she could stop it. But she meant it. With everyone staring at her, she gave the glass dish to Aaron. "Here, sweetie, take this inside. I'll see you later, okay?" She turned to Victoria. "It was nice to meet you.

I hope you enjoy your stay.'' She turned to Mike. "Drop dead.''

Her piece said, she turned on her heel and left. She stomped all the way back to her apartment. After letting herself in, she slammed the door with enough force to send a picture to the floor. The startling, jagged sound was good. She paced up and down the length of her unit, from the front door to her bedroom, and back. Hands fisted in rage and humiliation and embarrassment, she walked on, glaring through tears at the emptiness in her heart.

She would still have been pacing Monday morning if someone, about an hour later, had not banged on her door. Already on the return circuit to the front door when the knocking began, Julie stopped by her couch. *By God, it better not be him. Please, God, let it be him. See? See why you're pacing? See why you're so mad?* Julie raged to the door, jerked it open, confronted Mike, poked out her lip and grabbed him two-handed by the front of his jacket, hauling him inside.

"Julie, listen to—''

She slammed the door behind him. Another picture hit the floor. Strengthened by her anger, she forced him against the wall. His eyes widened in shocked surprise, but he didn't resist her. "Shut up. Just...shut up, Mike DeAngelo. Don't say a word."

She let go of him and stomped across the room. "I have never in my life been this angry, so I don't know what I'm capable of. Just tell me one thing—did you know your wife is *the* V. L. DeAngelo—the award-winning, world-famous photographer and writer? Did you?''

Mike pushed away from the wall. "Hell, yes. Of course I knew. And she's my ex-wife."

"Aha! Just as I suspected. If you knew, why didn't you tell me?''

"Tell you what, for crying out loud?''

"Who your wife is...was." She threw her hands up and resumed her pacing. *Men.*

Mike called after her as she neared her bedroom. "I did, if you'll calm down and think about it, Jul—"

Rounding her turn, she again faced him and strode stiffly toward him. "Oh, no, Mike. No. You said your wife was…skiing in Switzerland or something."

"No, I didn't. I said she was hang-gliding in Holland. She was."

"That's not much of a clue, buddy. I mean, V. L. DeAngelo? I've read her stuff. I've seen her pictures in art galleries, for God's sake. I cannot believe I did not put two and two together."

Mike stopped her interminable pacing by grabbing her arm when she paced by him. "Julie, I think I know what this is all about. Admit it—you're not this mad because my ex-wife is who she is."

She wrenched her arm free and stepped away from him. "Oh, yes, Mike, I am. I am this mad exactly because of who your ex-wife is. Trust me on this one."

Mike shifted his weight to his other leg and ran a hand through his hair. "Why? Why should it matter?"

That did it. Bam. Right over the edge. Julie stalked right back. "Why should it matter, you ask? I'll tell you why, Mike. Because I can't compete. That's why. I can't compete with your women. I mean, look at me."

She stepped back, looked down at herself and swept her arms wide. "Look at me. I'm just a middle-class girl. I'm not some great beauty. I'm not in the newspapers. My work doesn't hang in a gallery. I don't save unwed mothers and troubled youth. Oh, yeah—that's Caroline. Isn't she beautiful and rich and quite the humanitarian? I mean, Mike, where do you get these women? And how many is enough? I guess I should have known. A guy who looks like you— Men like you get women like them. But what I can't figure is, why are you with me? Am I just for convenience's sake? Is that it?"

Mike had his hands on his hips by this time. With his eyebrows drawn and his mouth firmed to a thin line, his face resembled that of a hawk—a mad-as-hell hawk. "Will you calm down and let me talk to you, instead of wallowing in this little pity party?"

"Pity party? Is that what you think this is?" Beside herself now, Julie stepped up to him again and poked her finger repeatedly in his chest. "All right, then, mister, I'll give you pity." Ignoring the burning tears in her eyes that blurred him, she said, "Look at me, Mike. Really look at me." She shook her head.

"What do you see? I'll tell you. A stinking yuppie. That's what. I'm not even thirty yet, but I have the MBA, I have the career in business, I have the BMW. Heck, I even have the clothes and the apartment. This year, next promotion, I'll even have the condo. And that's always been enough. Or so I thought. See, since college, I never let anyone close enough to get in my way. Not guys. Not even friends. Oh, I know a lot of people, sure, but they're not real friends. They call, they come over. But they're not close to me. But that's okay. That's what I wanted because my career always came first."

She saw a change come over Mike, a subtle hardening of his face. But she kept on going. "Achieving something in my life, on my own—that was important to me. And I've done it. I'm still doing it. I'm the baby in my family— and that's how they all still see me. The baby. Everyone has to help Julie. She can't stand on her own two feet. Well, I can. I've proved that. And I didn't need anyone else to help me do it. But you know what's left? A chocolate Easter bunny, Mike. The kind that's hollow on the inside."

"Hollow? The woman I held in my arms last night was anything but—"

"Shut up," she raged. "This is my pity party, remember?" The tears rolled unheeded down her face. "And then there was you." She gave in to a sobbing laugh before going on. "My mother brought me...you. I didn't know I was hollow inside until I met you and fell like a deflated blimp—smack, Goodyear hits the dirt. I opened my heart to you. Ha! I did more than that—''

Mike stormed to her, hauling her up against him. "I will not listen to you making yourself out to be cheap. I won't. You're not at all like you're saying!"

Julie wrenched free and stumbled back. "I'm like whatever I say I am. You can't tell me how I feel. You can't even tell me how you feel. And why not? Because there are too many women in your life. I can't fight it anymore, Mike. You see—and this is the funniest part of all—I love you.'' An anguished sob ripped from her heart. "Isn't that hilarious? I love you. For the first time in my life, I love someone. And I can't have him. That's hard for a spoiled baby like me to accept."

Mike started toward her. Julie put up a hand. "No! Don't touch me—please. You're not free, Mike. You have no right to touch me. You have Caroline—my cousin, whom I happen to really like. Now that I know her—thanks to you. And then there's V. L. DeAngelo. Your ex-wife. Beautiful, rich, self-assured, jet-set. Do you see the pattern here, Mike? I'm none of those things. I'm just…me. And I would never be enough."

Mike ran his hands over his face and then dropped them to his sides. His features were twisted with emotion. She'd won. He was defeated. Her heart ripped in two, like an unwanted Valentine. He turned away from her abruptly and made a ragged sound. Then he did an about-face. Decision was written on his ruggedly handsome features. Julie gripped at the cotton fabric of her couch.

"Julie, you are so wrong about me and about yourself that I don't even know where to begin. I—" He stopped and shook his head. "I'm not going to say any more. Not tonight. Look, Tory just left with Aaron. I can't think straight right now. Just let me say that I never meant to hurt you."

An unnamed but jagged emotion tightened Julie's chest.

"What do you mean, Tory just left with Aaron? Who's Tory?"

"My ex-wife."

"Why does she have Aaron? Oh, Mike, I—"

He put up a hand. "It's okay. She took him with her to Atlanta. Her parents live there. And it seems she's getting married again, too. To her editor." He laughed. "That is so damned perfect. I've met the guy. He and Tory are two peas in a pod when it comes to selfishness. They'll be very happy."

Rage and fear evaporated, leaving Julie feeling only concern. For Mike. "Are you okay, Mike? Is she…is she bringing—? Is he coming back?"

His face hardened. "Oh, yeah, he'll be back. A week's her limit for mothering. It's really okay. I've never kept Aaron away from Tory or her parents. It's hard enough on him without me adding to it."

What a screwy time for him to turn noble and selfless on her. Suddenly seeing herself through Mike's eyes, suddenly realizing how her tirade must have sounded to him, on top of everything else he'd been through tonight, Julie drew herself up. "Look, Mike, I know I've said some pretty selfish and mean things here tonight. I meant them. Well, most of them. But I want you to know that if there's anything I can do—"

"About what, specifically?"

Julie's heart leaped in her chest. His tone of voice left no doubt that he was hardening his heart, right along with his expression. All right. He'd closed himself off to her. Which was exactly what she'd meant to do herself, wasn't it? Wasn't saying goodbye—and meaning it—the only avenue left to them?

With regret thundering through her veins, Julie recanted. "Nothing, Mike. You've got so much going on in your life that the last thing you need is me complicating it further. Just know that I'm glad we had last night. I don't regret it. Not now, anyway. Maybe I will later. Who knows? But—"

And then she couldn't go on. Not with the painful lump clogging her throat. "Could you leave, please? I'd like to be alone now."

Mike didn't say anything at first. He just roved his gaze over her, as if memorizing her. Finally, he said, "That can be arranged."

He turned and, for the third time, walked out of her life at her own insistence. And this time, just like the time at her office, he didn't go quietly. No, he slammed the door behind him—the door that separated their worlds. Another picture bit the dust.

THE PHONE ON MIKE'S DESK rang Monday at midmorning. The same way it hadn't stopped ringing since he got here. He hit the blinking red button for his extension and picked up the receiver. "DeAngelo here."

He listened to Maureen down in the lobby tell him he had a female visitor. He looked at his watch. *Damn, that was fast.* He inadvertently cut the receptionist off before she could tell him the lady's name. "Yeah, I'm expecting her. Go ahead and sign her in. I'll be right there."

He hung up and came to his feet. "Hey, Sal, I gotta go downstairs and play escort. I talked with Mrs. Garcia over in Ybor City this morning. She's got one of those guys on her answering machine tape. She's bringing it to me. Pull her file, okay?"

Sal looked up from the overstuffed, open drawer of the filing cabinet he was sorting through. Like Mike, he was coatless, and his shoulder holster stood out in stark contrast to his white shirt. "What—that interstate fraud thing with the old folks?"

"Yeah. Damned scum. Taking those peoples' life savings and then cutting out on them. Guess it's Florida's turn to be involved. Maybe she's got something solid. Anyway, I'll be right back. Catch my phone, okay?"

Sal held his hands out as if he expected to catch a football. "Yeah, throw it here."

Mike slipped into his suit jacket, shrugging it over his own shoulder holster. He buttoned it while he stared at Sal. "Don't give me any ideas, partner. Not today."

As Mike was leaving their office, Sal called out after him. "Hey, DeAngelo, when you get down there, if it's really some well-endowed young chick, bring her up here and I'll…interrogate her for you, huh?"

Mike waved his hand without turning around. "Pig."

Sal got the last word in. "Oink!"

Shaking his head, Mike walked to the elevator. When the doors opened, he got in, pushed the button for the lobby, put his brain on autopilot and stared up mindlessly at the blinking numbers as the cage descended smoothly. If he allowed himself to think about his personal life right now, he might start running when he got out and never stop.

The doors opened and he stepped off. As usual, the lobby was crowded with people. Mike saw them as a blur, a backdrop, as he walked up to Maureen. He spoke first to the security guard next to her. "Hey, Connelly, what's new?" Then, turning to Maureen, a pleasant, efficient woman of about fifty with big hair, he asked, "Where's Mrs. Garcia?"

"Who?" Maureen pulled the pencil out of her graying hair, where she always kept it, and used it to scan down a sign-in sheet.

"Mrs. Garcia. You know—you called me and said I had a female visitor?" Mike moved around beside her to look over her shoulder.

Maureen's pencil stopped about three names from the bottom. "Ah, there it is. Cochran. She said it was personal. Anyway, I told her to have a seat over there against the wall. She's all badged and ready to go."

Mike tore his gaze away from the name written on the page to look at the receptionist. "She's really pretty."

His heart hammered. His gut felt like he'd been punched.

"Yeah, but you know you're the only woman in my life, Maureen."

The stout woman hooted her opinion of that and waved a hand at him. "Don't tell my husband that. Now, go on with you. The poor little thing's pretty nervous."

Mike winked at a grinning Connelly and turned to face the row of chairs that lined the wall. People crowded between him and Julie. Elevator bells dinged, hushed conversations swirled, doors opened and closed all along the corridor. But it was like he could smell her. He could have closed his eyes and walked straight to her. Within seconds, he was standing in front of her, and she was looking up at him. She laid aside a much-thumbed magazine.

He didn't say anything and neither did she. *Poor kid. She looked tired.* The mauve tint under her eyes told him she hadn't been sleeping. Mike cut his gaze down her in a sweeping glance. *Jeans and a sweater. On a Monday?*

"You're not working today?" He wanted so badly to trace the outline of her cheek with his hand.

She shook her head, setting auburn curls off in a swirling dance across the heightened color in her cheeks. "I called in sick."

He slid into the empty chair next to hers, taking her hand in his. "Are you really sick?"

She looked down at their hands. He followed her gaze and noted how his hand dwarfed hers, how her soft, slim fingers made his look rough and thick. "No. Yes. Well, in a way."

She looked up at him again, her heart in her warm, blue eyes. "I had to see you, Mike. I said some awful things—"

He tightened his grip on her, even as every instinct told him to let go. "Mostly about yourself."

She shifted her gaze to his tie tack. "I know. I'm such a jerk." She raised her head again. "Are you really busy? I mean, I know this is the FBI and all, but—"

He stood up, pulling her to her feet. "Yeah, I'm really busy. But I want to hear what you have to say." He let go of her hand to grip her elbow. "Come on, you're already signed in, you may as well come upstairs with me."

She hung back uncertainly. "Is it okay? It's kind of weird being here."

Mike grinned. "It's okay as long as you stay with me. Don't wander off, or someone might shoot you."

Her eyes widened in alarm. "You're kidding, right?"

Mike shrugged shamelessly. "I might be."

Julie molded herself to his side as he escorted her back to the bank of elevators. Mike fought the bittersweet feeling of having her against him. After this past weekend, he knew every inch of her. He knew her smell, her little sounds, her taste. He knew how to play her body like the fine instrument that it was. And he knew that she could bring him to his knees with one touch, one look. Just as he knew it was all so much more than the sum of any of those things, this whatever-it-was between them that was messing up both their lives.

Mike pushed the button and stood mutely by the woman he was coming to suspect that he loved. But was it enough? It hadn't been with Tory. Maybe he'd never really loved Tory, because what he felt for Julie was so different. Suddenly it occurred to Mike that Julie had a lot more in common with his ex-wife than he'd realized before last night. She'd given up everything else in her life to pursue her work, same as Tory. She'd pushed away the very people in her life who loved her, same as Tory. By her own admission, she'd let no one get between her and her career. Same as Tory.

Suddenly, standing there watching the floors tick off on the lighted panel above the doors, Mike began to cool. *What the hell was he doing? All right, DeAngelo—the truth. Admit it. It just might be that Julie will be the one woman you'll love for the rest of your life.* Just might be. No certainties in there anywhere.

Well, there was one. He wasn't prepared to give up everything he had with Caroline to explore what was really just a possibility. Or to put Aaron through it, either. The kid was just getting used to the idea of having a 'nother mommy. But, more than that, Mike knew he had a commitment to Caroline, and he would honor it. Hell, the wedding was less than two months away now. Things were starting to heat up. He stole a glance at Julie. She gave him a tentative smile. Yes, they certainly were.

8

"Hey, I was just kidding there, buddy. But thanks, all the same." Sal grinned hugely, looking like a tremendously pleased bulldog. He sat at his desk, unabashedly giving Julie the once-over. Finally, he scooted his chair back and stood. "This ain't who you thought you was going down for, is it?"

"Down, Pomerantz, and no, she isn't." Mike tightened his grip on Julie's elbow. He'd never hear the end of it from Sal after this. "Come here and be nice to the lady. And try not to scare her. Sal, meet Julie Cochran. Julie, this is my partner, Sal Pomerantz." He then leaned in close to her, speaking aloud but acting as if he were sharing a confidence with her. "Don't worry, he's housebroken."

"Call me Sal, sweetheart." Laughing, Sal gripped her hand in his huge paw, but turned his attention on his partner. "I like her." Without a pause, he turned his Brooklyn charm on Julie. "You forget this guy. He ain't nothin' but trouble. But an ugly guy like me? I'll treat you right. We could have beautiful kids together. Make your ma proud, I swear."

"That's it." Mike disengaged Julie's hand from Sal's. "Hey, can you give us a few minutes?"

Sal tore his grinning stare away from Julie's reddening face to turn to Mike. "Yeah, sure. I was just on my way out. You go to lunch before ten-thirty and you miss the crowds." He turned back to Julie. "Can I bring you something—a soda, a wedding ring? I'm serious here. Don't break my heart, Julie."

She grinned at Mike, and then at his partner. "Sure. I'll take both."

"Then, both it is." With that, Sal lumbered over to his desk, pulled his jacket free, shrugged into it like a circus bear and came back to Julie, taking her hand and raising it to his lips. "Parting is such sweet sorrow, my Julie...ette."

Mike rolled his eyes. "Shakespeare from you, Pomerantz? I'll have nightmares."

Sal laughed, and waved his farewell when he got to the door. "I'll ask Haney to get the phones for a while." He closed the office door behind him.

Grinning and shaking his head, Mike turned to Julie. "I can't do a thing with him."

She smiled. "I like him. I just might take him up on his offer."

"Great. The nightmare begins."

Julie laughed with him and then quieted, looking around the office. Mike tried to see it through her eyes. Crowded, cramped, cluttered. "It's not much, is it?"

She turned back to him. *Damn those eyes.* They were crystal clear and unfathomable. And yet he could get lost in them.

"It's enough. I think it's a good office."

Pleased by her answer, Mike leaned back against his desk and crossed his legs at the ankles. "Sal says we're too busy to be organized."

"I like that. You ought to have it done in needlepoint and framed."

"Maybe I will. I'll give it to him next Christmas."

Mike finally remembered his manners and offered Julie a chair. She sat down. And then it grew suddenly silent. Julie fiddled with her purse strap. Mike ran a hand through his hair and then rotated his shoulders, readjusting his shoulder holster under his jacket. Finally, he stood up and removed his coat, tossing it carelessly over the back of his desk chair.

Julie's eyes widened. "I guess I never thought about you carrying a gun."

"All the time. But don't worry. It's not loaded."

She looked from his gun to his face. "It's not?"

"I'm teasing you. Of course it's loaded." *How was it that one slender woman could turn him to mush?* Trained in hand-to-hand combat, firearms, terrorist tactics and interrogation, to name a few deadly arts, he still couldn't ask this one woman what she was doing here.

Julie turned abruptly to him. "Mike, I—" She just as abruptly turned away. Mike waited her out. She took a deep breath and swung back to him. "Mike, I was upset last night. More than I should have been, I guess. And I took it out on you. I'm sorry."

His heart screamed at him to take her in his arms. His head told him to stay where he was. He listened to his head. "You don't have to apologize. It's how you feel."

She shook her head. "No, it isn't. Not really." She looked at him, her heart in her eyes. "Mike, I have no right to say this, but I want to fight *for* you—not *with* you. But how can I? I don't know how you feel about things, about me. And last night, I—"

"Don't." He pushed away from his desk and drew her to her feet. Staring down at her, loving her, he reached up to tuck back a stray curl from her cheek. He then rubbed her jawline and spoke softly. "What am I going to do with you?"

Her face puckered. "Oh, Mike, I'm so sorry. I shouldn't have come, I know." When she tried to free herself, he tightened his grip. "I didn't mean to put you on the spot. I'll leave."

"No. Don't leave. Just give me a minute." He let her go and turned toward the window. Who was he trying to kid? He knew what he had to do. What he had to say.

Without preamble, he broke the silence. "My father was career navy—an admiral. We moved all the time. Home for me and Mom was wherever Dad's next duty station was.

It was okay. We saw a lot of places, did a lot of things most people don't get to see and do."

For a moment, she said nothing. Then she managed to say, "It sounds great. Where do your parents live now?"

Mike turned to her. She'd sat back down—on the edge of the chair, as if poised for flight. "Oklahoma City. I'm their only kid, which of course makes Aaron their only grandchild."

"And he's such a sweetie. They must miss him."

Mike realized he was staring at her. Forcing himself, he swiveled toward the window again. "Yeah. I take him there two or three times a year, or they come and get him. It's okay for now. But it won't be when he starts school, though."

Thinking of his son, just like he wanted Julie to do, Mike didn't say anything for a minute. He concentrated instead on the dull, heavy throbbing in his heart. When he'd collected his thoughts, he went on. "All my life, my father believed in honesty, loyalty, commitment, patriotism—ideals that are just given lip service nowadays. But he passed those ideals on to me. And I believe in those things. They're a part of me."

He heard Julie shift in her chair. But she didn't say anything.

Not daring to look her way, knowing he'd lose this battle with himself if he did, he trained his gaze down onto Zack Street and absently followed a random car on its course. When it rounded a corner, he went on. "The FBI is about those things, too. After I got my degree, I got recruited right out of the University of Oklahoma. Been with the bureau ever since."

"It suits you well. You're a man of integrity."

Mike gave a self-deprecating snort of laughter. "I used to be."

"What do you mean?"

He turned to her, leaning a shoulder against the wall. He put his hands in his trouser pockets. "I'm getting around to that. Tory and I met in college, got married after graduation. She started on her career in photography. There were good times. Then Aaron came along. But so did her big opportunity with the travel magazine and gallery shows, stuff like that. She decided she needed the acclaim and the excitement more than she needed us. So she split. Aaron wasn't even a year old.''

"Oh, God, that must have been tough. How could a mother leave her child like that?"

"That was pretty much my reaction. Since Aaron was born, I've been transferred from Atlanta to Boston to here. And he's not four years old yet. Its been tough on him, but he's a trouper.''

She sighed. "But now there's Caroline to be home with him. Isn't that what you want me to say?"

He straightened up. She was beginning to see the thread of this conversation. "I met her a little over a year ago. We started talking about kids. She's passionate about them, and we really hit it off. Then, about the time we got engaged, I got transferred here.''

"Good old Uncle Sam. He doesn't have much respect for relationships, does he?" She smiled, but hurt dawned in her eyes. "Do you love her?"

It was the same question he'd been asking himself lately. "I love a lot of things about her."

Julie cocked her head at him. "Heck, so do I. But that's not what I asked you."

Mike frowned fiercely. "I asked her to marry me."

"That doesn't count. Sal just asked me to marry him."

Like a cornered animal, Mike attacked. "Well, unlike you and Sal, Caroline and I are getting married." He hated himself when Julie's smile turned brittle, but he pressed on with his point. "And now you know about me. Honor. Commitment. Dedication to family. Three things Tory never had. Her career came first. It always did. She didn't let anyone—not even her son—stand in her way."

Julie quickly looked down, but Mike saw the wet brightness in her eyes. "Like me, according to you."

An act of sheer will was all that kept the wrenching pain in his heart off his face. "Like you. In some ways. In others, not at all."

"But in the ways that count with you?"

For two cents, I'd leap right out that damned window. "Yeah, Julie. In the ways that count with me, you remind me a lot of Tory."

She stood up abruptly, forgetting her purse. It hit the carpet with a muffled thud. "Do you care anything about me at all?"

He couldn't lie. "More than you'll ever know."

"Then, why won't you fight for me?"

"Who would I be fighting?"

She shook her head. "I don't know. Maybe the way you were raised? Maybe your own damned sense of what's right and wrong? What about what's right for me? For you? Doesn't any of that count?"

"This is what I am. My wedding is less than two months away, Julie. I can't just pull out. Not at this point."

Julie put her hands on her hips. Defiance rose in waves from her stance. "Why can't you? Is it honorable to marry the wrong person? Haven't you already done that once?"

Stung, Mike retreated to stubbornness. "I gave my word, and I'll keep it." The words hung in the air like a pregnant pigeon.

"Well, then, I suppose that's all that needs to be said. You love Caroline enough to let her raise your son. To me, that seems unfair to her. You also say you care about me. But not enough to be with me. So, what am I supposed to think? That I'm good enough for one night, but not for a lifetime because I work, like your ex-wife? You think all working women abandon their families? Come on, Mike, get real. God forbid there should ever be a breach of honor on your record."

She stepped over her purse and walked toward him. "I

hope you and Caroline are very happy. You'll understand if I'm not at the wedding?"

Mike wanted to rage, but how could he? He'd made his decision. "I don't want it to be like this. I swear I don't."

She laughed harshly. "How can I believe that, Mike? If you won't fight for me, then there's nothing left for me to say. Or do. But before I go, I just want to note two things here. One, we're nowhere near a rest room for this big moment. And two, I get to walk out on you for once."

JULIE MADE IT AS FAR as her car before she burst into tears. *What an idiot you are. What did you hope to accomplish by coming here?* She turned her tear-stained face away from the impersonal parking garage with all its accusing cars. Had she thought Mike would make some undying pledge of love to her and just toss aside all his plans? *Idiot, idiot, idiot.*

Pulling a tissue from her purse, she dabbed at her eyes. Then, leaning into her car, she folded her arms on its roof. Just as she lowered her head to the comforting circle they made, another wrenching sob escaped her, echoing sharply in the cement cavern.

"Julie?"

She stiffened and then spun around. "Sal!" She immediately wiped her eyes.

"You okay, kid?" He put a large hand on her arm.

She waved away his concern, even as she fought the quivering of her chin. "Yes." It came out all watery and sobby.

"No, you aren't. Come here to Sal." He opened his arms, offering comfort.

Julie hesitated only a moment before moving into his embrace. He felt warm and solid and…and big. Pressed to him, with her hands and her tissue over her face, her shoulders shook as she cried. Sal held her loosely, patting her back awkwardly and as gently as anyone of his size could.

Held by him, Julie felt like a child. Between sobbing bouts, she told him what had happened upstairs.

"There, there, Julie," he soothed, stroking her hair. "I think I need to kick me some Oklahoma cowboy butt. Would that make you feel any better?"

Julie nodded vigorously. "Y-yes. Can I help?"

Sal chuckled. "Sure, I'll hit him high, and you hit him low."

Julie smiled into his stiffly starched shirt and then pulled back. Sal loosened his hold, but still kept her in the circle of his embrace as he looked down at her and raised his eyebrows in question. Julie repeated her smile for his sake. "I feel better now."

"Yeah. The thought of a good beatin'-up always cheers me, too."

Julie laughed, despite herself. And then leaned forward to kiss Sal's cheek. She pretended not to notice the explosion of red on his face. "Thanks. You're a great guy, you know. Maybe I *ought* to marry you."

His brown eyes warmed for the barest of seconds, but then he released her abruptly and snapped his fingers. "That reminds me." He reached into an inside coat pocket and produced a small, clear-plastic ball from a gumball machine. Inside it was a shiny gold ring, fake stone and all. He held it out to her. "Here. I got you this. I got you a soda, too, but I drank it."

Julie fell in love with Sal right then and there. "Oh, Sal. It's beautiful." She put a hand to her heart and smiled, even as she blinked back fresh tears. "You shouldn't have."

He acted all fierce and forbidding as he laid it in her palm. "Go ahead—take it. It cost me five bucks' worth of quarters to get that."

Julie held the plastic ball to her heart and smiled up at the big, rough-hewn, warmhearted man. "I'll cherish it always."

Sal scowled fiercely and looked all around, as if hunting

for an enemy. "Yeah, well, don't wear it for real. It'll probably turn your finger green."

Julie grinned at that. "I wouldn't care if it did. You know, you're a very sweet man." She impulsively stepped forward and hugged him.

Sal squeezed her in a quick, gruff manner. "Don't be tellin' no bad guys I'm sweet or nothin', okay? I got a reputation to think of."

Julie raised her right hand. "I promise."

Sal grinned. "I knew you were a good girl."

"That depends on where you're standing, but thanks just the same." And then the moment stretched out. She didn't know where to look and noticed that neither did Sal. "Um, I've got to go now. I know you do, too. Just—well, just thanks, Sal. Thanks for being here. Mike has a good friend in you."

Sal shifted around and groused. "He won't think so when I take his head off in a minute for hurtin' a good woman like you."

"Like I said, you're a good friend. Goodbye, Sal."

"Goodbye, Julie." He gave her a small wave and then turned toward the elevators. Her heart full, Julie watched him for a minute. Almost to the elevator, he stopped and turned back to her. "For the record, I think DeAngelo is a fool."

"So do I," Julie called right back.

Sal grinned. "You gonna let him get away with this?"

Julie searched her heart. And surprised herself with what she found. "No, Sal. I don't think I am."

Sal laughed out loud and gave a thumbs-up gesture. "That's my girl."

9

"MOM, YOU STARTED THIS. And now you're going to help me end it." This phone call was a big step for her. Julie plopped down in a tired heap on her bed. Telling Sal she was going to fight for Mike was one thing. Doing it was another. So, no more two-day, hand-wringing, crying jags. Time to act.

"Started what?" came Ida's distracted response in her ear. "No, Jack, not that channel. Put it on eleven. I want to hear the six o'clock news. Just put it on eleven, please. I know I'm on the phone, but I'll be off in a minute. It's Julie."

"Mother, will you listen to me, please?"

"Your father says hello. And I am listening. Now, tell me, sweetie, what was it I started?"

"This thing with me and Mike. I want him, and I'm going to fight for him. Now, are you going to help me or what?"

"No."

The merest gust would have blown Julie over. She brought the handset into her line of vision and stared at it hard before putting it to her ear again. "Hello, I'm trying to reach Ida Cochran. Do I have the right number?"

"That's cute. You heard me—I said no. Caroline is family, and I won't hurt her."

"Caroline is fam—what about me? What am I?"

"That's different."

"Explain."

"Oh, Julie. Okay, you're my daughter. If I find you a

husband, that's fine. But if I take one from someone in the family, then everyone's mad and there's a family squabble.''

"There's going to be one, anyway, Mother. Right here— between me and you.''

"No, there isn't. It takes two to argue. And I'm not arguing.''

"Yes, you are.''

"No, I'm not.''

"Yes, you— Dammit, Mother—''

"Julie Marie Cochran, you're cursing. Do you want your father to hear you?''

"You're about twenty miles away, Mother. He can't hear me.''

"He can if I tell him.''

"Oh, fine. Never mind. I'll do it myself.'' She exhaled sharply and switched gears. "Anyway, I also called to tell you that I got my promotion.''

"Julie! You did? Oh, that's wonderful! I can't believe it! Let me go tell your father.''

"No, Mom, this is not a good—'' Julie again took the receiver from her ear "—time.'' She looked up at her long-suffering reflection in the mirror above her dresser and shook her head. "Ten bucks says Dad gets on the phone now.'' She put the receiver back to her ear and waited.

Bingo. "Hi, Dad. Yes, good to hear your voice, too.'' She looked at her reflection again and told it, "You owe me ten bucks.'' Then she turned her attention back to her father. "Yes, I know—I got that promotion. Yes, I'm very excited about it. I can always use the money. Yes, I'll invest part of it—

"What? No, not a party. Really, I don't want a party. Tell her no, Dad. When? Mom says Friday at seven o'clock here at the apartment clubhouse? And she'll make all the arrangements. What? Invite my friends from the bank?'' That was about fifty people. Julie rolled her eyes and gave in. No one but her mother could pull together a party of this size in two days. "All right, fine. Yes, everyone will come. They won't want to have to tell Mom why not. Oops, I have to go—someone's at the door. Look, I'll give you all my new-job details Friday night, okay? Yes. Love you, too, Daddy. Kiss Mom for me. Okay. See you then."

Julie hung up the phone. No one was at the door, but it'd gotten her off the hook. A knocking sounded at the front of her apartment. Okay, there was someone at the door. That'd teach her to lie. Rebuttoning her blouse, she padded down the hall and opened it. She froze in place, but her heart lurched. "Mike."

Leaning indolently against the jamb, his arms crossed over his blue-suited chest, he removed the silver-tinted sunglasses that hid his eyes. "Surprised?"

"Shocked."

He put his sunglasses in an inside pocket of his suit coat. "Can I come in?"

"No."

He straightened up. "Look, Julie—"

"No, you look, Mike. I made an ass of myself only two short days ago in your office. I've cried my tears, and I'm done with you."

She cocked a hip and crossed her arms, just to prove it. If only she could quit blinking so rapidly. And wondering what she was thinking of. She'd told Sal two days ago she was going to fight for him, and she'd just tried to enlist her mother in that same struggle. And now here she was saying she was done with him—and saying it to his face. What gives?

She watched him sweep her up and down with his black-eyed gaze. Then she got into a staring-down contest with him, barely managing to blink again when he gave her his verdict. "You don't mean that."

What gave him the right to be so darned sure of himself? She made a move to close the door. "Well, you're wrong this time. Because I am through with you."

Mike stopped the door with his hand. "I'm breaking off with Caroline."

It hit her like a ton of bricks. She should've been cutting a Woody Woodpecker victory dance all over the apartment, but she wasn't. She should've thrown her arms around Mike's neck in the throes of ecstasy, but she didn't. Maybe if Monday hadn't happened, this would be a touching moment. But Monday had happened, so instead, she stood there, doing a slow burn. "What does that have to do with me?"

A crease formed between his eyes as a frown claimed his face. He came inside and put a hand out to her, but didn't touch her. "Everything. I want to be with you."

Surprising even herself, Julie turned her back on him, taking a deep breath. When she whipped back around, he was closing the door behind him. "What brought on this sudden decision? On Monday, you couldn't stomach the thought of breaking a promise. Or of having a working wife. And you pretty much told me to get out of your life."

"Yeah, and Sal pretty much jumped in the middle of my chest about it, too. Anyway, I thought about everything you'd said. And what he said. And you're right, both of you."

Sal really had jumped on him about her? *God love that big teddy bear.* "I am? We are? Imagine that. Um, what are we right about? I just want to be sure here."

"About me marrying Caroline, and it not being fair to her. You're right. And Sal said if I lost you, he'd kick my ass—and then marry you himself."

Julie grinned and bit at her lower lip. A stray curl caught on her eyelashes. She swiped it away. "So, you're here because of Sal...in a way?"

"Hell, yes. You seen the size of that guy?"

Julie chuckled softly. "Yeah, but his heart's bigger."

"Sal's a sweetheart, all right. But I'm not really here because of him. I'm here because of you. And me. Us."

"Us? Don't you think you ought to talk to Caroline first before you go talking about an 'us'?"

"I thought you'd be glad."

"Glad? That you're breaking my cousin's heart? Why would I be glad? Especially when I got this today in the mail." She skirted the couch and picked up a cream-colored envelope from off the coffee table. She held it up for him to see. "You probably recognize this as an invitation to your wedding?"

Mike ignored the envelope. But he did unbutton his suit coat and loosen his tie, as if he were the man of the house, just come home. "Well, that makes it a little messier for me. Damn. Is getting this invitation why you're acting like this?"

Julie wanted to fling the fancy envelope at him. "What am I acting like?"

"Like you're mad as hell."

"I am mad as hell, Mike. I've been on an emotional roller coaster since I met you. I haven't even known you a month, and I've already told you I love you. Heck, I've already slept with you. I've thrown myself at your feet, chased you to your office, humiliated myself, and all to be—I don't know, what's a good word?—*spurned* by you not more than two days ago."

"Spurned?"

Julie stopped long enough to stare at him. "It means burned."

"I know that. I just haven't heard it used in a long time." He frowned, as if trying to recall exactly when he had heard it last.

Julie stepped up to cuff him on the sleeve with the invitation. "Concentrate, Mike."

He grinned at her and took hold of her arms. "I want to see if you're lying." With no further ado, he pulled her to him and kissed her. Soundly.

The invitation fell from her hand. Julie made a determined effort to keep her eyes open, her body rigid, her mouth closed and her heart unresponsive. Her supreme effort lasted about one second before she fluttered into his arms and pasted herself to him from lips to toes. *God, he felt wonderful and warm and solid, and smelled clean and musky and male.* She salvaged her pride by repeating, *I hate you, I hate you, I hate you, I love you....*

"No!" She shoved away from him and kept backing up until she figured she was at least out of arm's reach. Not for anything would she admit how wonderfully wet and tingly her lips felt. She swiped at her mouth with the back of her trembling hand. Quickly, she tucked it behind her.

Too late. Looking mighty smug, he folded his arms across his chest. "You were lying."

Julie threw her hands up in the air. "Lying about what?"

"About not caring about me."

Had the man suffered a minor stroke? "When did I say that? My life would be easy if I *didn't* care about you. But I do. And therein hangs a tale."

"Therein...what? Shakespeare, right?"

Had he—Shakespeare—just popped up in front of her in a puff of smoke, she couldn't have been more distracted. "Yeah, or Chaucer. I can't remember which." Then she heard herself. English literature—when her life was falling apart? "What's the point of this conversation?"

He grinned, like a five-year-old who knew a secret. "Me breaking off with Caroline to be with you."

"You look pretty happy for a man who's about to break a woman's heart. That's not very endearing, you know."

Mike sobered and ran a hand through his hair. "Yeah, well, I don't think I'll be breaking her heart. The differences in our two worlds are starting to show. We'd never make it."

Julie looked down and spied the invitation on the floor. Behind Mike, under his feet. *Lordy, the symbolism.* "Apparently Caroline doesn't know that yet. Because I got my invitation."

"She wouldn't do the actual sending. That's Reginald's

job. Maybe she forgot to send him a memo. Who knows? Or maybe she doesn't have anyone there with her, like I have you and Sal, to make her rethink everything that's important to her.''

"Maybe she doesn't." Julie stared at the envelope while she collected her thoughts. *Okay, here goes—the big test.* She looked up at Mike. And caught his heart in his eyes. Well, she knew how to douse that light. "I got my promotion. I'm now a vice president with First Southern Bank.''

The light faded. Julie's stomach dipped, even as he smiled and nodded at her. "That's great. I'm happy for you. I know you worked hard for it.''

Julie raised her chin another notch. "Yes, I did.''

He put his hands in his pockets. "I guess you can get that condo now. And your life will be complete, Ms. Easter Bunny.''

Okay, she'd started it. But now it was too intense, too close to what was really wrong between them. Afraid to go down that road, Julie pulled back, resorting to flippancy. "I sure as heck hope my life isn't complete. I think they bury you immediately after saying things like that over your dead body.''

Mike offered a halfhearted grin and took a deep breath. He then turned his head to look out the sliding glass doors to the descending darkness outside. Finally, he turned back to her. The look on his face sent icy fingers up her spine. His expression was so...final. "Look, Julie, I just want you to know that what I'm doing with Caroline—going up there and breaking off our engagement—has nothing to do with you.''

She swallowed the clumped emotion in her throat and forced her words out. "I'm glad. Remember, she's family. I wouldn't want to be the cause of a squabble.''

"Yeah, I can see how you'd feel that way. Anyway, I'm flying up to Boston on Saturday morning to tell her. Then,

Sunday evening I'm coming back through Atlanta to get Aaron at Tory's parents' house. And then I'll be home.''

When he stared at her without blinking, without seeming to breathe, Julie felt that chill wash over her again. "Go on."

"I want to know if you'll be here when I get back."

Julie cocked her head, feigning confusion. "Of course I'll be here. I live here. I can't get a condo that fast—"

"For me, Julie. Will you be here for me? Will you open the door if you know it's me? Will you take my calls at work? Will you…see me?"

Oh God, oh God. Here it was—the point of no return. Julie put her hands over her face and hunched her shoulders. *Why were life and love so hard?* Bringing her hands down, she choked back a sob, determined that she'd listen to her head and not her crying heart.

"No, Mike, I won't. I refuse to be your Rebound Woman. Men never stay with their Rebound Women. Not forever. They move on. I couldn't take that, Mike. Besides, you need some time alone. Time to—"

Mike exploded. "To hell with time, Julie! To hell with Rebound Woman. What I need is you. And not some women's magazine diagnosis. I know my heart and my head now—maybe for the first time in my life. And they both tell me I need you.

"Look at me. I can't even touch you now. I'm close enough to you to smell your heat. I want to devour you, and I can't even touch you. It's like there's this…canyon between us. Don't turn away from me now, Julie. I'm doing what you said on Monday—I'm fighting for you." He stared at her. "I love you."

He forced it out, as if it were a curse. Stunned, Julie couldn't even react. The little cogs in her brain locked, brought all systems to a halt. The seconds ticked by. Though wrenching emotion gripped her chest in its fist, she managed to whisper out, "Hurts, doesn't it? Now, please leave. Because we're not good for each other. Loving someone isn't always enough, Mike. Not for you and me.''

STANDING IN A GROUP of her friends, Julie dropped the conversational ball when Mike walked into the middle of her promotion gala Friday night. Either he was crashing the party, or her mother was involved. She turned back to Charlene. "Excuse me a minute. I have to go kill my mother.''

Charlene affected a pout, even as she raised her drink in a salute. "But, boss, you promised I could help.''

"Maybe next time.'' Julie spared her assistant a grin, but still kept Mike in her sights. While she watched, she saw her father greet Mike as if he were a conquering hero. *Et tu, Brute?* This whole party was a plot to kill her, just like Brutus and the Roman senators had murdered poor old unsuspecting Julius Caesar. And it wasn't even the Ides of March yet.

She wormed her way through the crush of her wellwishing friends, all of whom had a pat or a hug or a congratulatory word for her. But finally, Julie found the devious Queen Ida. And just in time, too. She grabbed her mother's arm, stopping her from further regaling two glassy-eyed, male VPs from the bank with the clinical details of Susan's pregnancy. Making her apologies to the two men, Julie dragged her mother off to a corner before hissing into her ear. "What is he doing here?''

"He who—John Carpenter or Hank Atchison? You work with them, so you tell me.''

"Not them!'' she shrieked and whispered at the same time. "Him.'' She turned her mother slightly and pointed toward the clubhouse's tiled-and-mirrored foyer. "Him!''

Ida clapped her hands together excitedly. "Oh, goody, he did decide to come. I knew you'd be excited.''

"I am not excited, Mother. Not.''

Ida pulled back from her daughter. "You asked me to help you.''

"And you said no.''

"Well, I changed my mind. You're my baby, after all, and—"

"And I don't want Mike, Mother. Not anymore."

Ida's eyes grew round. And her hand went to her pearl necklace. She absently fingered the beads as if they were a rosary. "Oh. Well, which is it? First you want him. Then, the next minute you don't—"

"Well, it's final. I don't."

"Fine, but you're telling him. Not me."

"Fine. I'll tell him." Julie put one foot in front of the other. *No problem. Get out, Mike. It was easy—*

Her mother grabbed her arm and pulled her back into their corner. "When I called Mike on Thursday to ask him to come tonight, he told me you two had words, and then he said he's flying to Boston tomorrow to break his engagement to Caroline. Did you know he's doing that?"

"Yes." She hissed the word out, but then she cocked her head in speculation. "Mike really talked to you about...us?"

"Yes, he did. And I feel sorry for him. Wait a minute—you know about him and Caroline breaking up?"

"Yes."

"Then, what's the problem? I thought you loved him."

"I do."

Ida shook her head. "That's it. I quit. Solemn vow on your Nana's head—no more matchmaking."

"That alone is reason enough for a party. But now, if you'll excuse me..." She looked down pointedly at her mother's hand on her arm.

"No. I won't let you hurt him."

"Mother, we've had this conversation before. I'm your blood, remember? Not Mike and not Caroline. Well, not Mike. Anyway, I'm the one you're supposed to worry about."

"And that's exactly why I'm not going to let you hurt yourself by pushing him away."

"Mother, I swear to you—"

"Hush. Here he comes now. And your daddy's with him." With that, Ida spun Julie around and finally released her arm. But apparently only so she could pinch her daughter. "Smile," she whispered into her ear.

Julie smiled through tears of pain in her eyes. Goose bumps traveled over her skin. Because of the pinch. Not because Mike was standing in front of her and mentally undressing her, with her parents only a foot away. Why did he have to look so handsome in a navy blue knit shirt?

"Look who I found, Julie—it's Mike! I practically had to throw cold water on that gaggle of females who had him cornered back by the bar."

"Mike," she gushed, playing the part of a snide, snooty woman to the hilt. "How nice to see you. I'm so glad you could take time out from your packing to come. You know exactly what your being here means to me—ouch!"

Had her mother actually pinched her on her bottom? Julie started to rub the spot. And got her hand swatted away.

Unsuspecting Dad to the rescue. "Mike here says he's flying up to Boston tomorrow. Can't wait until the wedding to see the little woman, huh, Mike? Mother and I got our invitations a couple of a days ago. We're really looking forward to the trip next month."

Ida stepped out from behind her daughter. She made an irritated gesture at the father of her children. "Oh, be quiet, Jack. There's not going to be any wedding."

"There's not?" He looked from his wife to Mike to Julie.

"No. Afraid not, sir."

To Mike again.

Jack patted Mike's shoulder. "That's tough, son. I'm really sorry to hear that. I was looking forward to having you in the family."

Mike's and Ida's gazes met and then swung immediately to Julie, as if this were a play and she'd dropped her cue. Julie burned under their pointed stares. For sure, the poor palm next to her was wilting. And it was artificial. "What?"

Mike held a hand out to her, wanting her to take it. "Can I see you for a minute?"

With her heart in her throat, she grinned as if rigor mortis had set in. When actually, panic had. "Why? No. You're seeing me right now—ouch!"

Ida innocently crossed her arms and smiled up at Mike. "She'd love to see you, Mike. Here, let me hold your drink." She took the beer from him and turned to her daughter. "Go with the man."

Excuse me, was she twelve or twenty-nine? But did she want to get pinched again? *Oh, okay. She'd go with him. Yeah. She'd go with him, all right. She'd show him the door.* She grabbed his hand, like she would've if he'd been a five-year-old who'd just belched, or worse, in front of company. "Let's go, buster. Me and you. Outside."

"Suits me," he drawled, and ended up being the one to drag her away. Big as he was, people just naturally got out of his way as he plowed through them.

Outside was just as crowded as inside. Mike took three steps in the direction of his apartment, but Julie balked like a Missouri mule. "No. I'm not leaving my party."

Mike looked down at her. He was not amused. "Fine. Then the rest room it is." He plowed right back inside and through the accommodating crowd, out the back door and down the narrow breezeway, stopping only when he reached the doors at the end. He tried one and then the other. Locked. *Ocupado.*

"Yours or mine?" Julie narrowed her eyes on purpose, to match the sneering lift of her lip.

"The first one that's free. Deal?"

"Deal." She tried to wrench her hand out of his crushing grip, but he crumpled her fingers even more tightly. Julie would have died before she'd admit that he was hurting her, the big jerk. *But once she got him in there—please,*

God, let it be the ladies room—she would give him a piece of her mind, boy.

A toilet was flushed. Mike looked down at her. This was it. A door was unlocked. Julie's heart beat in rapid protest to the suspense. The door opened. *Yes! The ladies' door!*

Out stepped Gina, one of the tellers. She was startled at seeing Julie and Mike hovering so close, but then she smiled. "Oh, Julie, we're all so proud of you—"

"Yeah, yeah. Excuse me, Gina." Julie took the girl's arm and moved her, none too gently, out of the way, so she could barge in.

Mike plowed in behind her and slammed the door. He let go of her to lock the knob and draw the bolt home across its catch. Then he turned to her.

At last. They were alone. *Now, to really let him have it.*

10

JULIE LAUNCHED HERSELF into Mike's arms. He caught her, crushing her to him, even as her legs went around his waist. She couldn't kiss him enough. And Mike was just as desperate. He turned them until Julie's back was against the gaily papered wall. Their frenzy of lusting and loving and twisting and groping knocked a dried flower arrangement off its nail and into Julie's hair. She helped Mike rip it out of her curls and hurled it herself to the tiled floor.

Her long skirt twisted up around her hips. Mike's hands followed it in hot pursuit. Her slip-on sandals hit the floor as she bucked against him and sucked in a breath. "This doesn't solve anything." *Was that gasping, panting voice hers?*

"I know. I know."

She kissed his mouth, his jaw, his neck, bit at him in little nipping kisses, ripped aside the open collar of his shirt. A button went flying when she tried to shove her hand inside. She wanted so desperately to feel the muscled plane of his chest. "Oh, Mike. We can't do this."

"I know. I know."

"No. You don't understand. We really can't do this." She clutched him to her—until he pulled her cotton sweater up and over her head. It went the way of her shoes, his button and the dried flowers. "You don't have…have protection."

"Yes—" he kissed her shoulders and undid her bra "—I do."

"You do?" Julie stiffened and pushed him back. Her bra

went with him when she levered herself out of his arms
and stepped back. The air-conditioning spilled a cool draft
over her bare skin.

"Yes." Mike stared at her, breathing heavily. He looked
like a magnificent, aroused stud. He ripped his shirt up and
off, tossing it over his shoulder. Julie found it hard to think
with his tanned, muscled, hair-fringed, exposed chest con-
fronting her. She focused, with no small amount of difficulty, on his face when he spoke again. "I carry one with
me now whenever I know I'm going to be around you. I
just can't keep my hands off you."

Had he not waggled his eyebrows at her right then, she
might have returned to sanity. And modesty. Not to mention decency. But he did waggle them. She held her arms
out. "Come here."

Mike's eyes lit with satyrlike glee. He finished undressing in Olympic-qualifying time. Within seconds, still in
contention for the gold, he had Julie naked, too, and in his
arms. The tiny room, however, presented its own unique
tactical and logistical problems. With Julie attached to him
like Velcro, her naked legs wrapped once again around his
waist, her arms around his neck, he cupped her bottom with
his hands and tried to turn. "How are we going to do this?"

Julie quirked her mouth up wickedly. "Try sitting on the
toilet."

He stopped his search for a likely spot in the room to
search her face. "Excuse me?"

"Put the lid down, silly." When his face still crumpled
in distaste, Julie chided, "All right. Bad idea. Who'd've
thought you'd turn out to be a prude? The sink?"

He turned until she could see it, too. *Hmmm. It was about
the size of a large soup bowl.* "Okay. Bad idea number
two. Got any of your own?"

"Baby, right now all my ideas are bad."

His words skittered over her nerve endings and plunged
to the quivering center of her. Lost to reason once again,

Julie sucked in a ragged breath and breathed out just as roughly. "Just do it, Mike. Now. Please."

"Whatever the lady says." With that, he backed her to the wall, raised her up in his hands and helped her position herself over him.

The slow, slithering slide down onto his hardness wrenched a ragged breath from Julie. Mike answered with a grunting moan, and Julie felt his hands on her bottom tighten convulsively. She smoothed her hands down from his neck, across the broad plane of his shoulders and down the diamond-hard aspects of his arms. "Love me, Mike."

He raised his head and looked deep into her eyes. Then, with utmost tenderness, he kissed her lips gently. Then with more hunger, more demand, more need. His tongue claimed her mouth, stroking in and out, wringing lusting little sounds from her. Soon, he started rocking, his hips against hers, a rhythmic rocking that drove her out of her mind. Julie could do nothing but let him carry her along on this passionate ride. Her back was literally against the wall, her legs entwined around his waist. He was completely in control. And she trusted him. Totally vulnerable, totally breached by him, she trusted him.

When Mike finally broke their kiss, Julie sucked in lung-filling breaths, convinced she was going to pass out. Mike was absolutely fierce tonight, as if he had to claim her, mark her as his.

Relentlessly he drove on, raising their shared heat to a fever pitch that tightened and twisted the bands of their desire. When finally the coiled dam burst, when finally their release came, Julie could do nothing but allow the shuddering ripples to claim her, to arch her back, to curl her toes. She became aware of his warm seed spilling inside her. Mike's seed.

Mike's seed? Ohmigod, ohmigod, he hadn't put on the condom! Ohmigod.

Julie struggled in Mike's slick and slippery grasp. She

shoved against his shoulders. "Mike! Ohmigod, the condom. You didn't put it on!"

Whereas Mike had just been slumped and soaked against her, he now snapped to attention. "Damn. I didn't." He snapped his gaze to her. "Damn it all."

Julie squirmed in his arms. "Put me down, Mike. Put me down. Ohmigod, we've got to think." She slapped his arm—hard. "How could you?"

"Ouch." Still, he loosened his hold. "I swear to God, Julie, it was an accident. Damn. How could I be so stupid?"

As if they were boxers retreating to neutral corners at the sound of a bell, they stood on opposite sides of the tiny room, separated by only about ten feet, staring and panting at each other. Julie spoke first. "Okay. This wasn't all your fault. I was the one who threw myself at you."

"Maybe, but I'm the one who's supposed to wear the condom. I am so damned sorry."

"No, Mike, it's not all your fault. I never gave you a chance."

"That's still no excuse. I'm the one—"

Julie held up a hand. "Stop. The blame game isn't solving anything. I have to use the toilet and…clean myself up."

As if this were an everyday occurrence in the Cochran-DeAngelo household, Mike unprotestingly went to the sink to splash water on his face and wet down paper towels, which he wiped over his sweat-slick skin. Julie took care of things as best she could. Once done, she sat down on the toilet seat resting her elbows on her knees, and shook her head. "This is not happening."

"Julie?"

She looked up through the wild tangle of her hair and saw that Mike was squatted down in front of her. He put a hand on her arm in a warm, reassuring gesture. "This is not the disaster we think it is."

Julie could only stare at him there in front of her, naked.

"This isn't a disaster because…? Mike, we just had unprotected sex."

Mike let out a breath, confirming the disaster. He took his hand off her and ran it through his hair. With one fluid, naked, Greek-god movement, he rose to his feet.

Now all the guy stuff was at her eye level. She looked up at him. "Would you mind moving all that equipment away from me for the moment, please? I've seen all of it I want to for one night."

Mike frowned as he looked down at himself. "I see what you mean." He leaned over to snatch up his briefs and tugged them on. "Better?"

Great. A muscled, tanned, Greek god in white cotton underwear. Damn him. He just looked more virile. Oh, don't even think that word. Julie moaned. "Yes. Much better. Now, hand me mine, please." She held her hand out limply, expectantly.

Mike turned until he spotted her lacy underwear. He bent down and picked them up, holding them out for her inspection. "Um, they're all tangled in that hootchy-thing that was on the wall."

Julie watched his fumbling efforts to sort tricot and lace from dead flowers and dried twigs. *How could this get any worse?* The fates answered her. The underwear snagged and tore.

"Oops." Mike looked at her, started to grin, apparently realized he'd better not, and grew solemn.

"Just hand them here, please."

He did, and Julie finished pulling twigs out of her panties. With studied slowness, she stood and drew them on. The tear revealed itself to be a vertical one, in the back, which halved her buttocks. *Lovely. Just like the butt's torn out of my life.* She looked over at Mike. He stood there, leaning against the wall, his hands behind his back, a study in guilt.

Julie crossed her arms under her bare breasts, and stared at him. "Okay. First thing. My period was…let me think."

No, let me slit my wrists. "Two weeks ago? More? You're going to laugh, but we women don't really keep up with that like we should."

Mike pressed his lips together and stared at her. "I'm not laughing."

Julie looked down. "Me, either. Look, I'm sure it's fine. All that…fertile stuff should've passed by now."

Mike nodded, as if he was waiting for her to say more. When she didn't, he jumped in. "All right, seeing as how this is modern times, we've got to talk other partners. I've had two in recent history—Tory and Caroline. You probably won't believe this, but both of them were virgins." He quirked her a go-figure look.

He'd found two gorgeous, adult virgins? was all she could think. Then her stomach plummeted when his expression revealed he was struggling with something. *Good God, what now? Was he going to tell her he's an alien and she now carried the hybrid link?* "What?"

What was troubling him finally came out all in a rush. "I think you deserve to know that since I met you, I haven't slept with Caroline."

Julie blinked several times. *In that case, who exactly was he cheating on—her or Caroline?* She took a deep breath. Her turn. Feeling hot and sweaty, she looked everywhere but at him. "Okay, me. In recent history for me—no one. Just you. I've dated, sure, but I never let anything get to the serious stage. So, there was no need for me to worry about birth control. You know that career thing you hate? Seems it's kept me pure."

"Look at us—the Switzerlands of the sexual revolution." Mike smiled at her. His smile was a little sickly, true. But it was a smile, nonetheless. He then brought his hands up to rub his face. "I'm so sorry for putting you through this. But it's done now, and it really isn't a disaster. We'll just have to be more careful next time—"

"If there's a next time."

He looked at her. Just looked at her. It gave Julie enough

time to trace that line of black hair down the middle of his belly until it disappeared into the band of his underwear. She resettled her gaze on his face when he spoke.

"I really don't want to discuss the future here in the ladies room while we're in our underwear, okay? Let's just get dressed and get out of here. I'll go to Boston tomorrow and come back Sunday with Aaron. Then, we'll take it one day at a time. I'll live my life. You live yours. And we'll see if they cross paths. Deal?"

There were fifty things she wanted to bring up that were wrong with his plan, but like he said, they were standing in their underwear. "Deal."

With nothing settled and with her heart heavy, Julie began to dress. She moved silently past Mike, or out of his way, when he needed to pick up an article of clothing or needed more room to put something on. And he did the same for her. There was no need for words now, no need for speed. And no desire for touching. The passion was spent. Reality was totally in control again.

It was only when she and Mike were fully dressed, and the dried-flowers-and-twigs hootchy-thing was once again on its nail, and there was nothing left to do but open the door and walk out, that something else occurred to Julie. She grabbed at Mike's arm when he reached for the lock bolt. "Mike, something's wrong."

He frowned down at her. "About ten things are wrong here. Can you be more specific?"

"Do you hear anything?"

He listened. "No. Why?"

She made an agitated noise. "Don't you think you should—like people talking and laughing and music playing? A party?"

His eyes widened and a nice pink color suffused his face and neck. "Uh-oh."

"Uh-oh is right. We've been in here a good twenty minutes or more. And women have pea-sized bladders. And yet, there hasn't been one knock at this door."

Mike frowned. "I don't want to go out there."

Julie laughed at his don't-make-me face. "If you think I'm going out there alone, you're crazy."

Now he pouted. "Well, you don't have to explain anything to anyone. You're a girl. This is the women's rest room. Now, me? That's another story."

"No—us. The two of us, plural, coming out of here together—we're another story."

Mike looked from her to the door. Julie followed his gaze. The door didn't flinch. When Mike's gaze swung back to her, Julie looked up at him and gave him a fatalistic, we're-dead-meat look.

"They're your friends. You know 'em—so do you think they'll do something to embarrass us...like applaud?"

Julie thought about that. "Oh, probably. I think at the very least they'll also rent one of those airplanes that trail streamers with messages on them, like you see at football games. I can see the message now—Mike and Julie, sitting in a tree, k-i-s-s-i-n-g. You know the rest."

"Yeah." He continued the schoolyard chant as if forced to. "First comes love, then comes marriage, and then comes Julie with the baby carriage." He looked at her. "Right?"

She looked right back. "Wrong."

He ran a hand over his mouth and shifted his weight. "Boy, this stinks. Why do we always end up in a rest room? I mean, Freud could probably fill ten volumes with this."

Julie quirked up her mouth and nodded in resignation. "True. But speaking of volume, let's go out and see why there's no music for us to face." She looped her arm through his, resting her hands on his solid forearm. "Shall we?"

Mike took in a deep breath and let it out in a long gust. "I want my mom."

Julie shook her head while he unbolted the door and put his hand on the knob. "And speaking of moms, Mike, mine will not be amused. She thinks I'm a virgin because I'm not married. And my dad will most likely have his shotgun and a preacher already waiting for us—just on the other side of this door."

Mike froze. "Could you possibly say or do anything more to make this moment harder or more awkward for me?"

Julie pretended to give his question serious thought. "No. That's it. I've got it all out of my system now."

"Thank God." He turned the doorknob. And slowly squeaked open the door.

Only to reveal to their peering eyes, not the leering, cheering, knowing grins, hoots, marching bands, shotguns or preachers they expected, but total and absolute... emptiness. Out in the breezeway, there was no one but the two of them and a few security lights that someone had switched on.

Julie turned to Mike. There was no need for words. This was weird. She knew it, and he knew it. Mike took her hand as they walked to the glass-paned doors of the clubhouse and peered in. "Twilight Zone" emptiness. Had Rod Serling begun talking, Julie believed that neither one of them would have jumped.

Mike tried the doors. Locked. The room, though darkened, still held the cheerful litter of the party. "Okay, where are they? They're not going to do something juvenile like jump out and say boo, are they?"

Julie looked through the clubhouse windows to the parking lot on the other side of the building. "I don't think so. The cars are gone."

Mike let go of her hand and turned to her. "Did we go through a time warp?"

Julie looked at her watch, and didn't feel the least bit silly doing so. "No. We entered that rest room less than thirty minutes ago. My guess is we were heard—we know we were seen. Remember Gina? And everyone cleared out so we wouldn't be embarrassed when we came out. Which is what we were. Right?''

"Oh, yeah, sure. Like you won't be mortified on Monday. I can't let you face that alone.''

Julie waved off his concern. "Don't worry about it. Time will have passed by Monday. My friends will be happy for me, the perverts. As for the rest of them—hey, I'm their boss now.''

"That's true. You're probably right, but I still don't like it. I don't want you to feel like I abandoned you.''

Julie laughed up at him, even though his darned sense of honor gave her a warm, fuzzy feeling. "Abandoned me? Are you the same brave guy who wanted his mother not five minutes ago?''

"Would you please be sure to bring up my shortcomings every chance you get? But that's another thing—where's *your* mother?''

Julie shrugged. "Probably helping Dad load the shotgun while they wait for the preacher. You might want to leave for Boston right now and not come back.''

THE STEADY DRONE of the airplane's engines as they cut through the air currents were reassuring and impersonal at the same time. Mike pushed back in his seat and adjusted the earphones that piped soothing music into his ears. He closed his eyes and laced his fingers over his abdomen. Thank you for half-empty flights. Because today he needed space.

Hell, after this trip he'd get all the space he needed. Mike pressed his hand against his roiling stomach. He hadn't even called Caroline to tell her he was coming. Was he hoping she wouldn't be around, and he wouldn't have to hurt her? No, he had to hurt her. Because being with her— no, being without Julie—was killing him.

Being *with* Julie could kill him, too. *Damn her for telling him to leave for Boston and not come back.* He ripped out the earphones and set his seat upright. Great. Now he was ticked off again. In his mind, he saw himself walking Julie to her door last night to make sure she was safe. Man, this sense of duty was stamped into his genes, wasn't it? Even when he was ready to choke someone, he was still the Upright Joe.

To hell with Julie. He wasn't doing this for her. For once, he was doing something for himself. And it felt pretty damned good. Liberating, in fact. Was this how women felt when they'd ripped off their bras in the sixties? Like he'd ever know. But he knew Julie was right about one thing. He didn't need to be involved with her or anyone else for a while, after ending it with Caroline. Julie'd said he needed time to himself. *Time to himself. Yeah. That sounded good.*

He picked up the earphones. Smiling smugly, he put them back in his ears and leaned back in his seat again. *"Solitary Man." Sing it, Neil Diamond. Me and you, buddy. Solitary men. Women—who needed them?* But before the song was done, Mike laughed out loud. He opened his eyes to see the curious stares of two flight attendants. He shook his head and waved off their questioning looks.

He closed his eyes again, chuckling. Julie's butt up in the air. Whenever he least expected it, there it was. Her naked butt up in the air that Sunday morning when she'd been looking for his boots and her entire family was there and he was stuck in that stupid bathroom…

A FEW HOURS LATER, Mike was in Boston. Thirty minutes later he was in the mansion-mausoleum-museum that served as the Wyndemere residence. And it was just him and Reginald at home. Mike stared at the slender, blond, elegant man seated in the probably antique-and-priceless chair on the other side of the probably antique-and-priceless little table that stood between them.

He'd bet Reginald knew the names for these chairs and that table. And probably knew their entire pedigree and history, or however furniture was graded that said it was too good for the average Joe. And another thing, how'd a guy get to be in his thirties, and still want to be called Reginald?

"We expect Miss Wyndemere back momentarily, Mr. DeAngelo."

Mike turned his best FBI stare on the man. The officious little twerp was so prissy and refined that he made Mike feel like a big, muddy puppy who'd just soiled the carpet. "Who's we, Reginald? Got a mouse in your pocket?"

Reginald breathed in audibly through his thin nostrils. "Hardly, Mr. DeAngelo."

You got anything at all in your pockets, buddy? When the heavy ticking of the antique grandfather clock over in the far corner of the football-field-size room nearly provoked Mike to a mindless act of violence, he spoke up. "Where'd you say Caroline was?"

Reginald crossed his legs like a girl. *Ouch.* He then flipped open the appointment book in his lap. Mike watched as Reginald ran a long, perfectly manicured finger down a page. "Yes, here it is. She's at a fitting for her...wedding gown."

Mike's stomach had the decency to do a guilty flop. Still, he managed to maintain a calm, smooth expression. But only until Reginald looked up at him and he caught a flash of naked emotion in the man's eyes. *Wait a minute.* Reginald hated him. Why? The only thing between them was Caroline—*son of a bitch!* Intuition flashed—*Reginald loved Caroline.*

Well, what do you know? Sure, he and good old Reggie had their turf battles over her in the past when it came to him loading up her schedule when he knew Mike was flying in, but he'd never suspected this. And come to think of it, Caroline clung to every word this pantywaist said. Mike nearly smiled. *Reginald Carston, I just might be making your day.*

Suddenly Mike felt like a granter of fondest wishes. Until the butler—Jeeves or James or Jerome or...something with a *J*—announced that Miss Wyndemere was At Home and Would Be Receiving Guests Momentarily. To Mike, everyone around here spoke in capital letters. And made him feel he wasn't good enough.

Or did he do that to himself? Hell, no, he didn't. Why else would Miss Wyndemere's fiancé be referred to as a guest? Well, to hell with them all. He was acting on his own behalf. Now and for always. That thought sustained him for the next few moments until Caroline swept into the room.

"Mike, darling! What a lovely surprise!"

Mike stood up. So did the impeccable Reginald. Mike watched the man's face when Caroline, a delicate study in silk and the finest wools, swept past her personal assistant to embrace her intended. And thought he knew how the man felt—he'd probably have that same look on his face if he had to watch Julie run past him to get to some other guy.

Caroline pulled back to smile up at him and cup his face in her hands. Mike couldn't shake the feeling that her happy surprise was just the tiniest bit forced. But maybe he was projecting that onto her, in light of his own guilt. Caroline turned to Reginald. "Reginald, was there some mix-up? Did I know Mike was coming today?"

Reginald stood there, his heart exposed to anyone with enough sense to see it. "No, Miss Wyndemere. This is a surprise visit. If you'll excuse me, I'll rearrange your appointments accordingly."

Caroline stared at him for one second too long. Mike felt the load on his own heart lighten. *She felt something for this guy. Good.* "Thank you, Reginald. But wait." She turned to Mike. "How long are you...can you stay, that is?"

No time like the present. "You'd better cancel everything, Caroline. For the whole weekend."

She frowned. *God, she was a lovely, elegant woman. And so wrong for him. Why couldn't he see that before now?*

"All right," she said slowly. "Mike, is something wrong? You look so grim."

Mike's gaze skittered from her face to Reginald's. The man was standing absolutely still. And made no bones that he was staring. Mike gave a barely perceptible nod to Caroline's assistant before shifting his attention back to his fiancée. He put his hands on her arms and rubbed them slowly. "Yeah, honey. Something's wrong. We've got to talk." He looked up to include Reginald. "Stick around, will you? Maybe in the next room or something?"

Fingers clutching whitely around the appointment calendar he held, Reginald moved only his eyes, sliding his gaze from Mike to his employer. "Miss Wyndemere?"

Caroline raised her chin a notch and put a hand to her throat, as if she were having trouble swallowing. But when she turned again to Reginald, her voice was steady. "If you would."

Reginald inclined his head deferentially to her and then gave a curt nod to Mike, laying on him a plain man-to-man look that said, "If you hurt her, you'll have to deal with me." Mike pulled himself up, as if physically signaling his rising opinion of Caroline's personal assistant. Mike held the man's gaze until he turned and left the room, closing the massive double doors behind him.

With nothing left to do but get it over with, Mike looked down at Caroline. Her sweet doe eyes and full lips turned up to him. A warm rush of emotion claimed him. He really did care about her. And he hated like hell doing this, but he couldn't shake the feeling he was correcting a wrong. "Why don't we sit down, Caroline?"

She remained statue still, except for her entwined, twisting fingers. "If you wish." She didn't move.

Mike, his hands still on her arms, led her over to the ornate Victorian sofa that held court in front of the fireplace. Sitting next to her, Mike half turned, resting his hand along the carved wood of the sofa's spine. It didn't help

his resolve any to see the tears already crowding her eyes.
"Caroline, I'm so sorry, honey. I never thought I'd—"

"Fall in love with Julie?"

Her words even shocked the grandfather clock. At least,
Mike couldn't hear it ticking now. But then again, there
was that roaring in his ears. "What?"

Caroline looked down. A tear splashed onto her hands
in her lap. "That's why you're here, isn't it? Because of
what you feel for Julie?"

Oh, boy. Now he felt like a dead rat in the punch bowl.
He took her hand. It was so cold. Like the area around his
heart. He let out his breath and spoke gently. "You picked
up on that, huh?"

She looked up, even managing a watery smile. Mike ten-
derly rubbed her tears away with his thumb. She stopped
his hand and squeezed it. "I'm not blind, Mike. Willful,
spoiled, yes. But not blind." She took a heaving breath and
looked him right in the eye. "Does she love you?"

Mike pulled his hand from hers and straightened up, facing the chairs that he and Reginald had sat in moments ago.
"I can't speak for her. She's mad at me for coming up here
and hurting you. And she won't talk about us—her and
me—until I…" He cut his gaze over to her and leaned
forward, resting his elbows on his denim-covered knees.
"She won't talk about us until I talk with you, and then I
have to be on my own for a while. Something about her
not wanting to be my Rebound Woman."

Caroline surprised him with a laugh. He turned to look
at her questioningly. "What?"

"I think you have met your match, Michael Edward
DeAngelo." Her smile was genuine, if sad. "I never was,
you know—your match, I mean. You're too strong for me.
You'd devour me with your zest for life…and loving. I do
love you, just as I love Aaron, but we're all wrong for each
other, aren't we?"

Her chin quivering, she looked down. When she raised
her head, there should have been a jeweled crown atop her

blond hair. "It was such a madcap affair we had, wasn't it? I've never experienced anything like it before. But what were we thinking, Mike?"

Never before had Mike loved Caroline more than he did at this moment. What a great lady she was. To be in a room with her was like basking in a royal presence. "We were thinking we loved each other, Caroline."

She smiled again, despite the pain in her eyes. "I probably always will. But sometimes that's just not enough to make a life together, is it?"

Mike chuckled at his own expense and shook his head, remembering Julie saying almost the same thing only last night. "No, I guess not. Women keep telling me it isn't, at least." He ran his gaze over the delicate features of her face. "You know you're the best, don't you, sweetheart?"

She gave a perky little shrug and then smiled, wiping at her tears. "Sure. Well, this certainly lets my tailor off the hook."

Impulsively, Mike leaned back and put his arm around her. It was over. It was done. Caroline cuddled next to him, her slim hand on his chest. "Your tailor? What do you mean?"

"Well, the dress was positively hideous today. It didn't hang right at all. I threw such a fit. Julie would have been proud of me."

Mike ducked his chin and shifted his shoulder, forcing her to look up at him. "Julie?"

Caroline's face was the dictionary picture of smugness. "Yes. She's all spit and fire. I think my spunky little cousin would have been proud."

Mike laughed out loud. "I know she would be."

Caroline sat up abruptly. Mike's hand went back to his lap. "Mike, if you marry Julie, we'll still see each other occasionally. We'll still be family, in some convoluted way. I'd like that. Would you? And I can still see Aaron. Say yes, please."

Mike held up a hand. "Whoa! Yeah, that's all fine with me. I just have to get Julie to say yes to me."

Caroline relaxed against the sofa's back, keeping her gaze on him. "Oh, she will. It's in the family blood to love you, you know."

The moment stretched out. Mike looked down at his hands and then rubbed his nose, not knowing what to say next. *Did he just get up and leave, or what?*

"You know, Mike, I've been thinking. I've decided not to let you off the hook so easily, after all."

Mike snapped to attention. "What do you mean?"

"When do you have to go home?"

"I'm picking up Aaron tomorrow afternoon in Atlanta. He's at Tory's parents' place. She's home from Holland and came to get Aaron for a week. She even met Julie."

Caroline grinned. "Oh, I'll bet that was amusing."

Mike laughed. "You don't know the half of it."

"Well, then, it's settled. You have until tomorrow afternoon. I want you to stay here and help me and Reginald deal with my parents and then undo all the wedding plans. There are scads of presents to be sent back, those damned invitations to be recalled, the church, the caterer, the poor tailor, the reception plans—all of it. I think you should share in that joy, don't you?"

Mike groaned, and slumped forward in exaggerated surrender. Then he straightened up and ran his hands through his hair. "Send in my man Reginald. I think we're going to make his day."

Caroline stood up and took Mike's hand to pull him to his feet. "I think we're more likely to ruin his weekend. All that work he's done on my wedding, and now it's all for nothing. He'll be livid."

Mike put his arm around her shoulders and shepherded her toward the ornate double doors. This Caroline and Reginald situation was something he couldn't wait to tell Julie—if she was still talking to him, that is. "Maybe not, Caroline. Maybe not."

She looked up at him, the self-conscious grin on her face accenting the deepening pink of her cheeks. "Why, Mr. DeAngelo, whatever do you mean?"

11

FROM INSIDE THE CLUBHOUSE, Julie looked out at the slashing rain. Behind her was a big plastic bag brimming with party debris from Friday night. You have the party, you clean up the mess. That was the rule. Dressed in her favorite pink sweats and white long-john shirt, she held her broom in both hands and just stared at the tennis courts as if they contained the answers to her problems. She turned her head, catching sight of two mighty oaks, draped in Spanish moss and fighting against the wind. To Julie, they looked like stout, gray-haired old ladies caught outside without their headscarves. Well, the weather was certainly appropriate for the first day of March.

She nearly crumpled in a pitying, whining heap. *Oh, sure, now you keep up with the dates.* By counting backward on her calendar, she'd realized her period started Friday the thirteenth, the day she met Mike. How many times had she scurried to the toilet today—less than forty-eight hours after "the incident," for crying out loud—to see if she'd started yet?

Get over it, girl. Clean up this pit and get back to your apartment. There's hot chocolate and a book waiting for you. Despite everything plaguing her, Julie smiled and indulged in a cozy little shiver. She'd picked up a new romance by her favorite author yesterday at the mall and couldn't wait to get to it.

See? Life goes on. Right in the middle of disasters, life goes on. Heartened some, Julie gave in to the seventies melody that spilled out of her portable CD player. She began sweeping with renewed vigor. *So where were her friends and family now when there was a mess here to be dealt with?* She harrumphed out loud. *Like I want to see any of them yet, after what had happened Friday night. Tomorrow was soon enough to be humiliated, thank you.*

She was glad she was alone. She needed to plot one Mike DeAngelo's death. *The wiener. If he were here right now*— Julie hoisted the broom as if it were a fencing weapon and made a few lunging stabs at the empty space she thereby designated as Mike. *"En garde, monsieur,"* she told the air in a bad French accent as she parried and thrust her way across the large room. "Defend yourself, or prepare to die. Ha! Take that. And that."

"And that!" a masculine voice behind her challenged as she was grabbed by the waist and swung up into the air. Her broom went flying, and she screamed out loud, clutching at the hands that held her prisoner.

"Put me down! Who—?" But she knew who. The only *who* who'd dare—the evil villain, Mike DeAngelo. She was spun dizzily again. Into her line of vision came the villain's sidekick, the giggling Aaron the Cute, who was clapping his hands gleefully and jumping up and down. "Put me down!"

"Okay." He put her down—with bone-jarring, teeth-clattering abruptness. And then spun her around to face him, holding her shoulders. "Did you miss me?"

When the three Mikes became one and her heart had gone from "racing" to "deliriously happy to see him," Julie found her voice. "Miss you? I haven't even tried to hit you yet. However, if you'll go stand out in front of my car, I'll—"

That was as far as Mike let her get before he grabbed her to him in a huge bear hug and covered her face with kisses, much to Julie's sputtering consternation and Aaron's screeching delight.

The little guy immediately attached himself to her legs,

and rested his head on her tush. "I miss-ded you, Julie. I was at my 'nother grandma's house in 'Lanta."

Pinioned in place as effectively as any Oreo middle stuff, Julie could move nothing but her head. "I missed you, too, Aaron. Did you have a nice time?" She twisted as best she could, trying to dodge Mike's continued kisses.

"Yeah. We had fun. An' my mommy was there. But hers gone now. She went to…um." He reached around Julie to pull on his father's jacket. "Where did her go?"

"Mountain climbing in Monaco."

Julie pulled back to stare in disbelief at Mike. "Do you make this stuff up? Mountain climbing in Monaco?"

Mike grinned down at her, as if she were a particularly wonderful Christmas package he'd just opened. "Swear to God, that's where she is."

"Uh-huh. Let me go, please." She wriggled in his grasp to prove she was serious. But Aaron was the only one who did as she asked. Julie twisted to see him scamper off and pick up a party hat she'd overlooked. When Mike loosened his grip, she looked up at him expectantly. But still he stared down at her, grinning. Julie cocked her head at him. "What is so funny?"

"You are. Was that me you were stabbing with your broom?"

Her gaze flitted around the room, settling everywhere but on him. "No."

"Liar."

She snapped her attention back to him. "I am not a liar."

"You're gonna go to hell if you keeping stacking 'em up, girl."

She renewed her struggles. "See you there, then. Now, let me go."

"Yes, ma'am." And then he opened his arms with a grinning suddenness that sent Julie stumbling over her own feet. Mike stopped her fall with a hand on her arm.

Julie wrenched free and swiped her hair out of her eyes. "What are you doing here?"

Mike raised an eyebrow and then looked around the room. "I live here."

She suddenly remembered a certain conversation in the rest room at Nana's party. "Not here, Mike. And don't start that. I mean, what are you doing here…with me?"

He grew serious. This particular expression of his somehow always emphasized the lean hollows under his high cheekbones. And made his eyes seem darker. He shoved his hands into his back pockets and shifted his weight. "I can't be anywhere but where you are, Julie."

She swallowed hard, feeling her blood course through her veins at a carnival-ride pace. If she weren't careful, he'd sweep her right off her feet. She looked down, and then over at Aaron by the back doors. He was wearing the party hat and sitting cross-legged on the floor, humming to himself and flipping through a magazine. She looked back up at Mike. "How's…how's Caroline?"

Mike studied her a moment and then nodded. "Caroline is fine. Turns out the butler did it."

"What? The butler?"

"I'm just kidding. I've always wanted to say that. But it turns out she loves her personal assistant. Remember Reginald—?"

Julie shoved at his chest. "Get out! Caroline and Reginald? Are you making this up? Because I swear if you are—"

Laughing, Mike grabbed her hands. "I'm not. How could I make up some soap-opera thing like that? Oh, by the way, she sends you her love. And says congratulations."

Julie frowned. "What? Congratulations? What for—? Oh, you mean on my promotion?"

Now Mike looked serious. He let go of her and snapped his fingers. "Damn. I forgot to tell her about that."

Julie thought she could still feel his strong grip around her wrists. "Then what for?"

Now he grinned. "For us."

"Congratulations for us? What are you talking about?

We haven't done anything—'' her face exploded in red-hot heat ''—well, we have, but surely you didn't tell her...''

Mike made a contradictory noise at the back of his throat. ''Hardly. No, she said congratulations on...well, winning me, I suppose.''

''Winning you? She said congratulations on winning you? Excuse me, I need my broom.'' She stalked around Mike and picked up her make-believe fencing sword.

''Hey, you're not going to use that on an unarmed man, are you?''

Julie hefted her weapon of choice until its weight felt right in her hand. ''Oh, yes. I am. I most certainly am. Winning you—ha! I never heard such self-centered conceit. Prepare to defend yourself, sir.''

Mike laughed and took one giant step toward her, handily disarming her. ''I *knew* it was me you were killing. How come?''

Julie folded her arms under her breasts. ''On principle, mainly.''

Mike absently twirled the broom between his hands, watching its motion. ''And that principle would be...?''

Julie took a big breath and let it out. ''Making me love you.''

The broom clattered to the tile floor. She had Mike's full attention. ''Why is that so awful?''

Julie shook her head, feeling bested, somehow. She glanced over at Aaron. He was rolling around on one of the brightly upholstered couches, lost in some imaginary game. She looked back to the boy's father. ''Because...because we're not right for each other, Mike.''

He narrowed his eyes. ''How the hell do you figure that?''

Julie made an imploring gesture. ''You don't want a woman with a career, Mike. And I won't give mine up.''

''No one is asking you to.''

''Come on, Mike. It's not that easy. Look, I'm not sure I want to do this...this you and me thing, okay? You may be sure, or think you are, but I'm not sure that you're sure. Does that make any sense?''

"No. But, look, Julie, I haven't asked you to marry me. All I'm asking is for you to give us a chance. I agree with what you said a few days ago. I need to be alone to figure out what's going on inside me. Just don't decide anything right now.'' He stopped, looking at her as if he expected her to say something.

Julie couldn't.

He nodded in resignation and went on. "All right. I did a lot of thinking on the airplane. And I realized that all you and I do is fight or make love, or both. We've never tried just getting to know each other. We jumped right into being lovers. Don't get me wrong—that part is great.'' He grinned at her, devastating Julie's defenses, if he only knew it. "But what I want most right now is for us to be friends—friends who happen to love each other. I've never had that with a woman. And twice in forty-eight hours I've had two different women tell me love isn't enough. I want to see what else there is.''

My God, what a beautiful speech. Julie was lost in his wonderfulness. *Then why in the heck are you saying no to this man?* He was the one she would love for all her life. She knew that. Just as she knew she would sacrifice her career, her apartment, her car, her clothes, her dignity, her freedom, her heart, her soul—you name it, for him. And now he wanted to be friends.

As her love life flashed before her eyes, Julie nodded. Now that she'd got what she wanted, what else could she do? "You're right, Mike. On all counts.'' She held out her hand. "Friends?''

He gave her that white-teethed, dimple-cheeked, dazzling, sexy grin of his that unhinged her knees...and then took her hand. Raising it to his lips, he kissed it. "Friends.''

"FRIENDS? YOU'RE freakin' friends with Julie now? I ain't lyin' here, DeAngelo, I can't keep up. You axed your wedding to Caroline four days ago for this girl. I thought you loved her."

Mike held his steak sandwich up in both hands and looked at Sal. "I do. Friends can love each other." He took a bite, laid it back on the plate in front of him, and then picked up his glass of iced tea.

Sal watched him chew. Then, eyebrows raised, he gave Mike a sidelong glance over the top of his meatball sandwich. "We're friends, Mikey. So, do you love me, or what?"

Mike thumped his glass down on the table and swallowed with great difficulty. "Don't make me slap you, Pomerantz."

Unoffended, Sal shrugged and took a huge bite. Wiping at his mouth with a paper napkin, he said, "Just checkin'."

"I'll give you something to check."

Sal's huge chest shook with suppressed laughter. But then he sat up straight. "Hey, this means Julie can wear my ring now, seein' as how you two's just friends and all."

Mike rested his forearms against the wooden edge of the table and leaned over the booth as far as he could. "Your ring, Sal? Your ring? You gave Julie a ring? What the hell are you talking about?"

Sal smirked. "She didn't tell you about that? That means it must mean something to her. Go figure, eh, Mikey? A good-lookin' guy like you, and I'm the one she—"

"Explain the ring, Pomerantz."

Sal grinned like a bulldog eating briars and took another bite of his sandwich, chewed it thoroughly, wiped at his mouth several times and kept a steady, cheerful gaze on his partner.

Five more seconds, Mike thought, *and then I'll kill him, right here in the restaurant.*

Finally, Sal swallowed and leaned toward him. "Excuse me, Mr. Federal Agent, but you're scarin' me with that face of yours." Then he sat back, waving away Mike's intensity. "It's nothin'. I'm yankin' your chain. Me and Julie's just friends. Like you and Julie. But unlike you, I bought her a ring—a gumball ring. That's all. It made her feel better.''

"A gumball ring? What the hell's a—? When?''

"That day she came to the office, and you made her cry.''

"Son of a bitch.'' But Mike wasn't talking to Sal. He was looking down at his plate, his appetite gone. His curse was self-directed.

"Yeah. I thought so, too. So'd she.''

Mike looked up. Sal apparently still thought so. "What the hell am I going to do, Sal?''

Sal's bushy eyebrows went up. "What do I look like here—Ann Landers? All of a sudden I know so much about women. It ain't like I'm your mother or nothin'. Hey, where you going?''

Mike stopped in his headlong flight out of the small diner to turn back to Sal. "Pay the bill, buddy. I'll get it next time. I gotta go make a call.''

His completely baffled partner gestured at him, obviously forgetting he still held his sandwich. A saucy meatball went airborne into the next booth and onto a startled woman's lap. Sal never missed a beat as he leaned over to the lady. "Sorry, ma'am. Official government business. Send Uncle Sam your cleanin' bill.'' He turned back to Mike. "Who you callin'?''

"Julie's mother!''

"OKAY, HERE'S WHAT WE'RE going to do.''

She was like a general on the battlefield, Mike mused as he stared in open admiration at Ida Cochran. She sat hunched over a legal pad and a calendar at her dining room table in Sun City Center that evening. She scrutinized her work, made a face, scratched out what she'd just written and started over.

"Okay. We need an excuse for the party. A theme or something. Got any ideas?''

Mike thought a moment, staring at her hands. She had a

ring on almost every finger. "No. Nothing. Unless you count the Ides of March, when Caesar was killed. That's in less than two weeks."

She consulted her calendar, wrote that date down, stared at it and then scratched it out. "No. It's too…serious. Besides, Jack looks terrible in a toga."

Despite himself, Mike began to get a mental image of bandy-legged, paunch-bellied Jack Cochran in a toga. "I see what you mean. But now I'm stumped."

"Me, too. Let's get Jack in here. He's overdue for a good idea."

Mike bit back a grin as she called her short, squat husband into her presence. Jack came in with Aaron. They each held Lego creations of their own. "Jack, honey, we need to celebrate something."

Jack fitted a tiny Lego onto his…thing he'd made, showed it to a very impressed Aaron, and then raised his blue-eyed gaze to his wife and Mike. "Yeah? Like what?"

Ida made a noise. "That's what I'm asking you."

Jack's expression slipped. "What? Did I forget something? It's not our anniversary, is it?"

Ida gave Mike a will-you-look-at-what-I-have-to-deal-with-here look. Mike clamped down hard on his back teeth to keep from laughing. She then turned to her husband. "No, it isn't, and you didn't forget anything."

"Good." Jack then inspected Aaron's conglomeration of plastic blocks. "That's pretty good, little fella. But I think you need a specialized gazinta piece. It gazinta this right here." He pointed out Aaron's engineering mistake to him. As the concerned little guy jetted off to amend his oversight, Jack turned to his wife. "So what do you want from me?"

"Jack, don't make me snatch out the last blond hair on your head. I'm trying to help Mike here with Julie. You know that."

"I do. Which is why I'm entertaining Aaron in the other room." His expression then sobered as he turned to Mike.

"And I'm hoping that this celebration has something to do with a future wedding. Especially after last Friday night's performance. Never again do I want to slink out of a party, along with a room full of amused strangers, because my single daughter's in a public rest room with a man and they're…you know."

Ida threw her hands up. "For Pete's sake, Jack, get with it. This is the nineties. Did you think Julie'd get to age thirty and still be a virgin?"

Mike's eyes widened. Julie would die if she heard this. He wasn't too sure he'd live through this conversation, himself.

Jack smacked his hand down on the polished table. "I know the times, Ida. But I'm talking to the young man here." He turned to Mike. "I'm asking you, so I can sleep at night. Until your wedding night, don't lay a hand, or anything else, on my daughter. You make that solemn vow to me, I'll help you. You break that vow, I'll break you. We got an understanding?"

Ida shook her head. "Now you're going to break him. He's got thirty years and fifty pounds on you. But all of a sudden, you're a Mafia don."

Keep his hands off Julie? Impossible. Several really hot and steamy images of her sweet, naked little body and of the two of them entwined in bed flared like fireworks through his libido. But wait—wasn't that exactly what he and she had decided last Sunday between themselves? Friends. No lovemaking. No fighting. Just getting to know each other. He refocused on Jack Cochran. The fireworks fizzled. "I promise, Mr. Cochran. I won't lay a hand on her until her last name is DeAngelo. If she'll have me."

Jack thought about that and finally uncompressed his lips. "She'll have you. You just have to convince her. I know my daughter loves you, or we wouldn't be having this talk. But I also know she takes after her mother. Stubborn? Let me tell you! The girl just wants you to woo her, like I had to do with Ida. So, I'm saying I've been there."

He pulled out a mahogany chair and sat down. "All right, what about Melba's kid's birthday on the twenty-third?"

Ida smiled, patting her husband's arm affectionately. "Glad you joined us. But that's too far off." She turned to Mike. "Melba is Jack's first cousin, and they live in New Jersey."

He nodded. And realized how much he missed his own parents, seeing these two loving people together. His folks were pretty upset with him for breaking off with Caroline. He'd called them last weekend, and it had not gone smoothly, to say the least. But before they'd hung up, they'd come around, telling him they understood. But he knew better—they didn't. They cared a lot for Caroline. But wait until they met Julie. There was no one like his redheaded, long-legged little friend, who would be giving them more grandchildren in the near future, if he had anything to say about it. When Jack tapped at his forearm, Mike jumped guiltily, sure the man had read his mind. "Sir?"

"We were just saying what about Saint Patrick's Day? She'd never suspect a thing."

Mike looked at Ida. She ran a finger over her calendar, located the date and raised her head, a green party already shining in her eyes. "It's staring me in the face, if I'd only looked. The seventeenth is on a Tuesday, so I'll make it an early buffet, and everyone can wear green. It'll be fun."

Mike winked at her and then grinned at Jack, holding his hand out to be shaken. "Mr. Cochran, you're a genius."

He shook Mike's hand and turned his dancing eyes to his wife. "You hear that, Ida? I'm a genius. Now there're two people who think so—me and Mike."

Ida pursed her lips and shook her head. "Just be glad you didn't have to wear a toga again, Mr. Genius. You make a much better leprechaun."

"I GUESS YOU HAVE TO GO."

"I guess I do." But Mike didn't move.

Julie and Mike had managed to get through their first official date—and hadn't ended up in a washroom! Mike was really trying this friendship thing. But now, as she stared at him, Mike's black eyes—*she'd swear to God*— actually turned up at the corners, making him look like some kind of satyr. His ears even seemed pointed. *Ohmigod, he's the big bad wolf in Little Red Riding Hood. Hadn't he called her that when he was in her bed—not more than several yards away?*

"I guess you have to go so your baby-sitter can get home." *Was that automaton's voice hers?* Julie crossed her arms over her blouse-covered breasts, hoping Mike wouldn't notice her suddenly attentive nipples.

"Yeah, I have to go so my baby-sitter can get home." His voice sounded just as tinny as hers had.

She could feel it—he wanted to grab her and make mad, passionate love to her. And, boy, did she want him to. *But friends didn't do that. They talked and got to know each other.* Okay. She could do that. "You want me to walk you home?"

Mike cocked his head at her. He smiled. "You know, I think I do." He crooked his elbow as an invitation for her to take his arm.

Okay. This was doing something. This was good. "That night air felt kinda cool. Let me get my sweater."

Quick as a blink, Mike ripped his maroon sweatshirt off over his head and held it out to her. "I'm too hot right now. Wear mine."

Julie stared at his broad, muscled chest, covered now only by a crew-neck T-shirt, and willed herself not to pass out. *This was not good.* "Okay."

She reached out and took the warm garment from him. Slipping it on over her white blouse and jeans treated her to the warm and heated scent of Mike DeAngelo. The sweatshirt was huge, and she smoothed it down, taking care not to do so in any suggestive or erotic way, thinking Mike was closer to being a charging, rutting bull than he was a gentleman. The sleeves hung past the tips of her fingers and the hem was halfway to her knees. She looked up at him as she rolled up the sleeves. Her hands stilled as she noticed the transfixed look on his face. *Oh, he liked her in his clothes. He liked it a lot.* Julie swallowed, hoping her lascivious thoughts would go the same way. They didn't. "Are you ready?"

His black-winged eyebrow rose evilly. "Oh, yeah, baby, I'm ready. This ain't a gun in my pocket."

Julie breathed in sharply. "Um, um, I guess we ought to go."

"We ought to goddamned do something." Mike shifted from one cowboy-booted foot to the other, and then reached up, in obvious and sheer distress, to run both hands through his hair. Seeing the flexing muscles in his arms, his expanding chest and concave belly above his Levi's that tautened his thin cotton undershirt, Julie brought her fingers to her mouth.

Turn around and open the door. *Turn around and lock the damned door before he gets out.* Julie jerked around and ripped the door open. "We've got to go—now! Before we do something we'll be sorry for."

Mike slumped and he let out an audible breath. "You're right." He strode purposefully by her, out of her apartment and into the breezeway before turning back to her. "You still coming?"

She wasn't sure, all of a sudden. Was she strong enough to be in his company for even the few minutes more it'd take to walk him home? Then she looked at him, at the clear pleading in his face, and gave in. "I'm coming. I always walk my dates home. I wouldn't want anyone to accost you."

"Gee, thanks, big, strong lady. I feel safe when I'm with you."

Julie poked her tongue out at him and grabbed her key ring from off the end table by the door. Stepping outside, she closed the door behind her and jiggled the knob to be sure it was locked. It was. *As tightly as a chastity belt.* She turned to Mike and smiled...sort of. "Okay. Let's go."

Within a few seconds, Mike had his arm around her. His wrist dangled over her shoulder and his hand hung loosely above her breast, but not touching it. Feeling safe and warm with him so near, Julie smiled into the darkness that enveloped them like a heavy blanket. *She was walking Mike home. How funny was that?*

"Julie, remind me, the next time I see your father, to tell him how much I hate him."

12

"ALL RIGHT. WHAT'S YOUR favorite color?"

"Purple. Look! There's Aaron up to his neck in those plastic balls."

Mike looked and waved at his son. "Yeah, he loves all this play stuff here." He turned back to her, censure clear in his expression. "Did you say purple?"

Julie frowned in defense of her answer. "I'm a redhead. I look good in purple. Not everyone can wear it."

"Not everyone wants to. What's your favorite ice cream flavor?"

Not for the first time of late did she sense something more here than met the eye. Julie turned her full attention on the FBI agent sitting next to her at the indoor playground. "Mike, why have we been playing twenty questions since you got back from Boston? We have been together every evening, and it's the same thing—more questions. I'd think you'd've asked these easy ones first."

"Just answer the question, ma'am."

Julie sighed. "Mint chocolate chip."

Mike pulled back and really frowned. "That's disgusting."

In a pout, Julie crossed her arms. "You don't like my favorite color. Now it's my ice cream. See? I told you we have nothing in common."

"Sure, we do. When's your birthday?"

"I've already told you. I remember saying it. Oh, okay. September 25. That makes me a Libra. I was born right here in Tampa, graduated from Brandon High School and earned my degree in marketing and my MBA from the University of Florida. Which makes me a Gator. There. Feel better?''

"Some. What's your blood type?"

"All right, that's it. Mike, you're beginning to sound like my mother.''

He looked offended. "I'm going to pretend you mean that in a nice way.''

"Well, I don't. The only thing you need is a legal pad and rings on every finger.''

"That can be arranged. Okay, a few more questions." He leaned in toward her. "Do you sleep in my sweatshirt you never gave back?''

Julie nearly slid off the chair. "Don't go down that road, friend Mike. Do you want it back?''

He smiled—no, leered—at her and sat back up. "Fine. Don't tell me. And no, I don't want it back. You keep it. Back to the questions. How much vacation time do you have coming to you?''

"What? Where'd that come from?''

"Just answer the question. It's important to my plans.''

"Your plans? Maybe I have a plan, too. Like maybe I plan to ask you a bunch of personal questions.''

"Fine. My birthday is November 4, and I'll be thirty-two. My favorite color is blue. My favorite ice cream is *plain* chocolate, like any normal person's. And my blood type is A-negative. Feel better?''

Julie narrowed her eyes at him. "You'd better tell me what's going on, Mike.''

He grinned at her. "Okay, vacation time? Come on, Julie, we're getting behind here.''

She surrendered. The man was relentless. "Well, you know me—Ms. Workaholic. At least, I was before I met you. I mean, here it is seven o'clock on a Thursday, and I'm not still at work. Any other time I would be. Okay, okay, I'm getting there. Keep your pants on.''

"It's getting harder every day to do that. Now, once again, vacation time?"

Julie thought about it. "Probably more than six or seven weeks."

He frowned. "Damn, it's a good thing I came along to give you a life. Okay. What's the bank's maternity-leave policy for its executives?"

Julie couldn't find her voice for several, very long seconds. Did he know? She sat up straighter, all the while denying to herself that her face was heating up nicely. "Gee, why do I think you have some hidden agenda here, Mike?"

"Beats me. Your face is red. Now, answer the question, ma'am, or I'll be forced to put you under a bright light and get out the brass knuckles. You know they're standard government issue."

"Yeah, I know. I watch TV. All right, quit frowning like that. Three months. New mothers get three months. Now, why would you need to know that?" Julie was afraid she'd have to take advantage of that company perk before very long. She hadn't had her period yet. And not even a blessed cramp to cheer her.

"Three months? Damn. If I had to push a watermelon out my—well, I couldn't, could I. But anyway, I'd want to lie around and gripe for about a year. You women must be tough."

"We are. Tougher'n you guys'll ever be." Julie really did not want to talk about motherhood. How was she going to tell him—especially if they decided not to be together? And even if they did, would she always wonder if it was because she was pregnant? What then? And why were they even having this conversation? He didn't want a working wife, and she wasn't giving up her career. *Hello, deadlock.*

In a dire effort to change the subject, she remembered something he'd said on their first "date." "By the way, you never have told me why you hate my father. What'd he ever do to you?"

Mike sat up straight and looked like a little boy caught with his hand in his mother's purse. "Nothing."

Julie laughed. He was so big and strong and handsome and virile—and yet could be so endearing. "Yeah, right."

"Okay, the truth. I hate him for having such a frustrating daughter. There. It's out."

Julie twisted her lips. He was lying, and she knew it. Now, how to find out the truth? *Aha. Two can play this game.* "That's not what Sal said."

Mike jumped up. "What the hell did Sal say?" His yelling drew the attention of every man, woman and child in the indoor playground.

Julie cut her gaze from Mike to look all around them. She smiled at their audience and shrugged her shoulders. Waggling a finger at him, she gloated shamelessly. "Sal hasn't said a word. I just wanted to see if there was something there. And apparently, there is. So spill your guts, DeAngelo."

Mike sat back down, leaning forward in his seat and peering intently into her face. "We have to get to know each other, remember?" He lowered his voice. "No sex, no fights—just friends."

"That's what all this is about?" Suddenly, it was heart-warmingly funny. Poor guy. He was burning up for her, but sticking to his word. *How sweet. How torturous.* Then, Julie really looked at him. There were deeper hollows than before under his cheekbones. He looked a little thinner, but it was hard to tell under all that muscle. Could it be that he hadn't shaved today? Darned if he didn't need a haircut, too. The man was falling apart. On account of her. *Good Lord, she was killing him.* She reached over to him and put her hand on his. "Mike, you are the biggest sweetie I've ever met."

He stared at her hand as if he'd just found a wonderful treasure there. "No, I'm the horniest sweetie you've ever met."

Julie gave a tiny shriek and covered his mouth with her hand. "Mike DeAngelo, there are children present."

He lifted her hand and ran his tongue along her palm. Julie jerked her hand away and stared wide-eyed at him for about ten seconds. Totally captivated and totally willing to be ravished, she intoned, "My middle name is Marie. My favorite movie is *Monty Python and the Holy Grail*. I love to read romances. I love chocolate more than breathing. I'm not afraid of bugs, even spiders. I have a terrible temper and hate to lose at sports. And once when I was ten, I spit on my friend, Beatrice, and threatened to pull all her Barbie doll's hair out if she told. There. You know everything about me. Can we go to bed now?"

It was Mike's turn to stare wide-eyed at her. Suddenly, he burst out laughing, and not two seconds later, he grabbed her and wrapped her in his ironclad embrace, thoroughly kissing her. When he released her, within a second of them forgetting themselves and disrobing, their parting was punctuated by a deep and abiding silence all around them. Julie turned with Mike to see everyone—everyone!—staring at them.

Mike darted her a look and then stood up. He opened his jacket and pulled out his badge, holding it up and showing it all around. "It's okay. I'm with the FBI."

"AND THEN HE SAID, 'It's okay. I'm with the FBI'. There was no one close enough to see if he really had a real badge, but they scattered, anyway. I swear, is that the funniest thing you've ever heard?"

Rosie, Sal's latest flame and Julie's new friend, laughed for a minute and then crossed her arms. She'd certainly taken Julie's hint to wear green to her parents' party tonight seriously. The woman looked like an exotic parrot, but a cute one. "God love him. But I have to tell you. The funniest thing I ever heard was when Sal—he told me this—was at lunch a couple of weeks ago and got to gesturing at Mike with his meatball sandwich. He ended up flipping a meatball onto a lady in the next booth and told her to send her cleaning bill to Uncle Sam!''

Julie, a green plastic bowler hat on her head, stared at Rosie and then they both killed themselves laughing. "I swear, Rosie, where do we get these guys?"

Rosie waved a hand dismissively. "Eh, they're government issue. There's a factory in Jersey that churns them out. I'm just glad I got me one. Did he tell you how we met? He brings some suspect into the hospital when I'm on duty. Turns out she's pregnant. OB got called. I went down with the doctor. Kismet, huh?"

Her emotions at war, Julie smiled and nodded. She had no desire to hear the word *pregnant*. Slamming the lid on that thought, she focused on Rosie. Mike had told her that Sal and Rosie were quite the item now, since their shared first date with Mike and Julie. Rosie was so pink and fiery and petite, like an opal, next to Sal's big diamond-in-the-rough personality. "I love Sal, don't you? He's such a big sweetie."

Rosie continued placing shamrock-stamped paper plates, cups and napkins around the huge mahogany dining room table at Julie's parents' home. "Yeah. He thinks you hung the moon, too. He told me about the ring he got you. Don't you just want to chew this guy up?"

Julie held her hand out. "Look. I'm wearing it."

Rosie grabbed at her hand, turning it this way and that as she admired the gumball ring. "Hey, just in time for Saint Patrick's Day. Look. It's turning your finger green."

Julie laughed. "Yeah, that's why I saved it for today. Oh, and thanks for coming early to help set things up. Mom hardly ever gets in over her head with a party, but this time, I don't know. She's acting all flustered and nervous about something."

Rosie shrugged. "It's okay. It's nice to be included. Being single isn't all it's cracked up to be, is it?"

"No." Julie looked down at the punch bowl into which she was pouring ginger ale over lime sherbet. A sudden lump in her throat made her swallow hard. She fought the welling tears, but feared she was losing.

Rosie moved to her, putting her hand on Julie's arm. "Hey, kid, what is it?"

Julie looked up, quickly swiping at her tears as she glanced over her shoulder toward her mother's kitchen and then back at Rosie. She moaned. "Oh, Rosie, what am I going to do? I'm pregnant. I did a home test, and it's positive. And, worse, Mike doesn't want a working wife. And I just got promoted to a vice presidency at my bank, and I won't give that up. And I can't—"

"Come here, honey. That's enough. Don't worry." Rosie, shorter than Julie, still enfolded her in her arms and patted her back as she rocked slightly. "I don't think you have a thing to worry about. You want the baby?"

Julie nodded.

"Okay. I'll put you in touch with a good doctor. Hey, you love Mike?"

Julie nodded even more vigorously.

"See there? Those are all the ingredients for a happy ending. Have you told him yet about the baby?"

Julie shook her head.

Rosie laughed. "Women's lib. Go figure. Nothing's changed between men and women, has it? My advice is, don't tell him. Not yet. Wait until after the party, okay?"

Julie nodded slowly. But wondered, what difference would it make—before the party or after the party? The problems were still the same. But somehow, the thought of putting off the inevitable, even for a few hours, appealed to her. Mike may as well have a good time, even if she couldn't. She'd tell him he was going to be a father— again—later tonight. Or maybe tomorrow. Or the next day.

Rosie bumped her shoulder up, forcing Julie to raise her head. Rosie held on to her arm with one hand and reached up to straighten Julie's askew little bowler. "Now, go dry your eyes and pretty yourself up. This is going to be a great night. I just know it."

"Oh?" Julie wiped gingerly at her eyes, trying to avoid smearing any more mascara onto her cheeks than was probably already there. "And just how do you know that? You sound pretty certain."

Rosie shook a finger at her. "Oh, no. You're not hearing it from me. Now, get yourself and your makeup into that little bathroom I saw off the kitchen and fix yourself up before you have to explain why your face is such a fright. They'll think this is a Halloween party, for crying out loud."

When Julie didn't move, but looked instead at the half-completed punch, Rosie gave her a gentle shove in the right direction. "I'll finish here."

Julie smiled at Rosie and gave her a quick hug. "I think this is the beginning of a beautiful friendship, Rosie. Thanks for listening." When Rosie waved her away with a dimpled grin, Julie quickly turned and grabbed her purse.

Avoiding the kitchen exit from the large dining room, she turned instead to her right and tiptoed down the terracotta hallway to the tiny half bath wedged in between the coat closet and a guest bedroom. *Damn.* The door was closed. She tried the knob gingerly. And locked. *Now what?* Julie bit at her bottom lip and looked around. *Well, what are you thinking? Like there isn't a mirror in the guest bedroom.* She had just started in that direction but the bathroom door opened up. *Of course.* "Mike."

"Hey, good guess." He looked at her face. "What's wrong? You look like you've been cry—"

"No, I haven't. Are you through in there?"

"I might be." He stood in the doorway and crossed his arms over his neon-green knit shirt and equally bright green-and-white shamrock-patterned suspenders. They looked wonderful with his white pants. And green socks. And white shoes. "Why were you crying?"

Julie took a deep breath and resettled her one shoulder pad that felt like it was bunched up inside her kelly green dress. "You don't want to know. Now, will you please let me by?'' Turning to the side, she tried to wedge her way in with her shoulder.

"Hey, don't let me stop you." He stepped aside when she shoved past him. And stood there staring at her.

At the mirror, she groaned at the sight she made with mascara smudged under her eyes. Opening her purse, she cocked her head at him. "Do you mind?"

He straightened up and took hold of the door. "My mistake." And then stepped back inside, closing it behind him. He pushed in the lock button and turned to her. "Better?"

Julie gave a heavy sigh. "I meant from the outside."

"And I mean to find out why you were crying."

"Well, I don't intend to tell you. Not yet, anyway. Right now I'm going to fix myself up. You can stay and watch. Or you can leave." That said, Julie focused on her reflection in the mirror. The moment was here, he had every right to know, and yet she just couldn't get the words out. Rosie'd said wait, and so she'd wait. So there. *Cop-out*, screamed the little voice in her head. *Shut up.*

"I'm staying."

Holding a moistened tissue to her eye, Julie turned slightly. "Suit yourself."

"I will." He squeezed by her to sit on the lowered toilet seat.

Julie removed the cap from her pencil liner and looked down at Mike, sitting sideways and looking up at her, completely fascinated, apparently, with this totally feminine business. "Could you maybe move in a little closer, Mike? I still have enough room to move my elbow."

"Sure. No problem." He grasped her hips, moved her out, swung his leg in front of her and then moved her back in, wedging her between his thighs. "Is that better?"

"I was being sarcastic."

He grinned up at her. "And you did it very well. What's that thing you're doing now?"

She looked from his face to her own hand. "It's an eyeliner pencil. Surely you've seen one before?"

He pretended to search his memory. "Possibly. So why were you crying?"

Julie leaned over to him to put her nose right to the tip of his. "Because you won't ever let me be alone in a bathroom. Happy?"

He reached up with both hands to cup her face and give her a quick peck. "No. So why were you crying?"

"Because you won't quit asking me questions. You're making me crazy, Mike DeAngelo."

"Good. Because you're keeping me awake nights, Julie Marie Cochran. I'll tell you how many cold showers I've had to take in the past few weeks, if you'll tell me why you were crying."

"That's it." Julie pulled her nose away from his and straightened up. Wedging away from him, she went toward the door and opened it. With her gaze on Mike, she ordered, "Out."

"Oh, there you are, Mike."

Julie jumped about ten feet and jerked around. "Mother!"

"Well, don't blame me. I was just passing by. I've been looking everywhere for Mike. I should have known you two'd be in a bathroom somewhere. Mike, Sal's eating cookies in front of your son and now Aaron wants one. Can he have a shamrock cookie?"

"Is there another kind tonight?" The big jerk just kept his smart-aleck grin on Julie and then winked.

Tugging on the jacket hem of her green polyester pant-suit, Ida made several sideways stabbing motions with her head, as if telling him to come with her. "Can I see you a minute, Mike? It's about the, uh, cookie thing with Aaron."

Some little light bulb dawned over his head apparently, judging by how animated his face suddenly became. And, whereas Julie hadn't been able to budge him, he jumped right up and went with Ida, barely nodding to Julie as he brushed past her. She shook her head and closed the door behind him. And locked it. Men. And mothers. Sheesh.

After repairing the damage, Julie surveyed her reflection in the mirror, made a face and went to the closed door. With her hand on the knob, she took a deep breath, let it out slowly through pursed lips, told herself to just get through the night, and then opened the door.

Only to come face-to-face with a big, green bulldog holding a fistful of cookies and leaning against the opposite wall. Sal Pomerantz. He held out a frosted shamrock. With his mouth full, he asked, "You want one?"

Doggone him. She couldn't even see him without wanting to kiss his forehead and smile. "Sure."

"Mike sent me to see why you were crying. He says you'll talk to me." He swallowed, took another bite and waited.

Julie fingered her cookie and grinned hugely. "You know, he probably didn't want me to know that he told you to check on me."

"Yeah, well, who cares? Especially if he was the one who made you cry. I already owe him an ass-kickin' for the last time." He looked down at her hand. "Is that my ring?"

Julie held her hand out for him to see. "It certainly is. Pretty, huh?"

Sal took her hand and rubbed at the green discoloration around her finger. "Pretty cheap, is more like it. So, what're you cryin' about? And don't lie to Uncle Sal here. Me and you, we got a history with this cryin' thing of yours, remember."

Julie shrugged her shoulders and stared down at her cookie. Finally she nibbled a bite off it and looked up at Sal's rugged face. He watched her with a depth of emotion that warmed Julie's heart. "I wish I could tell you, Sal, but I have to tell Mike first. It's only fair."

"Oh, so now we're bein' fair. Yeah, well, fair was me gettin' to be his best man when he was goin' to marry Caroline. You know you cheated me out of a trip to Boston and then home to Brooklyn?"

Julie bit at her bottom lip and then offered a bright smile. "Tell you what, if I ever get married, you can be my best man, okay? Or my maid of honor. Would you like that?"

Sal shrugged his massive shoulders and looked up and down the hall before resettling his gaze on Julie. "If the dress fits, I'll wear it."

Julie chuckled, and then changed the subject. "Hey, Sal, I really like Rosie."

"Yeah, me, too. I think I'll chase her until she catches me."

"Good. I'm happy for you." Julie felt a warm rush of affection for this man. Why couldn't it be this easy with Mike? "You know what? I already feel better, just talking to you."

He smiled. "That's the old Pomerantz magic." Then he turned serious. "Julie, if there's ever anything you— Well, you know."

"I know." She took his hand and squeezed it. "Now, come on. Let's go join that party. It sounds like about fifty people have shown up since I went into that bathroom."

"Yeah, and they're all green."

Julie looked at his outrageously bow-tied and checkered outfit and then down at her own costume. "Unlike us, right?"

Sal straightened up, feigning outraged dignity. "Hey, we're the epitome of high fashion here. Come on—" He put his huge arm around her shoulders. "Let's go show these people how to party until we're green around the gills."

13

IT DIDN'T TAKE JULIE more than a couple of hours to get green around the gills. The noise, the crush of the crowd, everybody and everything's greenness, the food, the combined body heats and perfumes, the music. She'd never been bothered by those things before. So maybe it was the pregnant thing playing on her nerves. All she knew was she'd needed to get away for a few seconds, to just sit somewhere quietly and breathe in and out.

When she came back into the room from her tenth trip to the washroom, she looked around. Mike was sorting through CDs with Sal, Rosie, Charlene and some of her other friends from work. Several people from the apartments were out on the patio talking and laughing with some folks from church. Huddled around the green buffet were chattering guests from about three different generations.

Over on the couch, Mom was sitting with Dad, holding court. It always amazed Julie that her mother could bring together such a diverse group of people who really didn't know each other at all, for the most part, and it always worked out. *What kind of party would she have when she found out her daughter was an unwed mother?*

Okay, time for a breather. Before she could be seen and drawn back into the crowd, Julie bypassed the living room and continued on down the long, darkened hall to its end and eased open the door. Peering into the semi-darkness, lit by a shell night-light, she found that the little mound on her parents' king-size bed was Aaron. Moving to the bed-

side, she leaned over and smoothed back the black hair
from his little baby forehead.

He mumbled in his sleep and turned over onto his back.
Julie pulled her hand back and held her breath. Aaron slept
on. She smiled down at him, wanting to pick him up and
hold him to her. He was precious, and so much like Mike.
And yet he was his own little man, too. She could listen to
him prattle on all day.

Someone behind her gripped her shoulders. Julie's breath
caught. But a soft, warm breath on her neck shused her,
even as she was pulled back against a broad, familiar chest.
"It's just me. I saw you come down the hallway. Cute kid,
huh?"

Julie relaxed against Mike, covering his hands with hers
when he wrapped his arms around her waist. "He sure is.
You make pretty babies, Mike DeAngelo."

He kissed her neck and whispered, "I want to make
pretty babies with you, Julie Cochran."

Oh God, oh God, oh God. Julie fought the tensing in her
muscles, forced herself to remain calm. *Tell that to her
heart.* "Well, we can't," she whispered back over her
shoulder. "I work, remember? And we're just friends."

"Outside," Mike breathed into her ear. He withdrew the
warm comfort of his arms from around her and took her
hand, leading her out to the hallway. Once he'd eased the
door closed behind them and looked up the hallway, apparently wanting to be sure they were alone, he put his
hands on her arms and looked down into her face.

Julie's heart pounded with the rhythm of the music fil-
tering from the party. *Tell him, tell him, tell him,* her conscience demanded. "Mike, there's something I need—"

"No. Me first, okay? For the past few weeks, I've been
hounding you with questions—small questions, questions
that matter, answers that matter, things we had to know
about each other. But there's something more important I
haven't asked you yet."

Julie frowned. "I don't think I got all of that."

Mike looked confused himself. "Me, either. Anyway, what I'm trying to say is—" He quickly looked over his shoulder and then back at her. "We don't have much time here before the cakes are presented, so what I mean is—"

"The cakes? What cakes?"

Mike exhaled roughly in exasperation. "Don't interrupt me or this whole thing'll go bust. Now, here's the thing. I don't care if you work. I want you to work. Your work is who you are. I'm a big jerk for ever thinking otherwise. I realize now—my enforced celibacy has cleared my brain— that it was never Tory's work that pulled us apart. It was Tory's…um, what can I call it? Her self? The way she's made? See, I blamed her job, saying if she didn't have that, she'd've never left. But I know now that's not true. She would have left, anyway. And for the right reason—she and I just didn't love each other enough. I mean, it just wasn't there between us. See what I mean?"

Julie frowned. "I think so. Go on."

"Okay. And with Caroline, I was just doing what I thought was best for Aaron. Don't get me wrong. I had, and still have, some feelings for her. But she and I know we were fooling ourselves, calling our friendship love. Because that's what it was—friendship. So I didn't love her, either, really, in the right way, the only way that counts."

"What…" Julie swallowed the hard lump in her throat. Was he getting ready to tell her he didn't love her, too? "What is the only way that counts, Mike?"

He gripped her tighter. "The way I love you, Julie. All my life, I've been looking for you. And I've made a lot of women miserable while I tried to find you."

Julie's heart hammered. "What are you saying, Mike?"

He smiled, his heart and hope reflected in his eyes. "I'm saying I want you to marry me, Julie."

Okay, it's a line from really old movies, but it fits here. "Mike, this is so sudden. I don't know what to say."

"Sudden? How can this be sudden? I've been going around for weeks with a part of my anatomy hard enough to cut diamonds every time I even think I can smell you, and you say this is sudden?''

Julie put a hand to her mouth to stifle the giggles. When she got hold of herself, she told him, ''I mean, we've only known each other for about six weeks.''

''How long is enough, before two people know it's right? Two months? Two years? I've known forever. Somewhere deep in my heart, I've known since the first time I saw you.''

Julie blinked rapidly to clear her vision. ''Mike, are you sure? I mean, you were engaged to someone else two weeks ago. How can you know that what's in your heart now won't change in a month?''

''It will. It'll be stronger.'' Mike let go of her to step back and run his hands through his hair. ''I'll grant you this much—I've been a mixed up son of a gun where women are concerned. But I know this is right, Julie. I know it. You are the one, the only woman I'll ever want. Hell, just look at me. I've lost ten pounds, I forget to shave, and I'm dressed in green and white—for you. I hate green and white. What more proof do you need? I'm a man in love.''

Julie's heart started to bubble over with joy. ''I've seen you wear green before, Mike DeAngelo.''

''All right, I lied about that. So what do you say, Julie?'' He looked again over his shoulder and then turned his avid gaze back on her.

She tried to look around his bulk. ''What is going on out there, Mike?''

''Nothing.''

''Liar. It's gotten awfully quiet.''

''No, it hasn't.'' He barely kept a grin off his face.

''I swear, you are the worst liar.''

''You should be glad. When I'm eighty and tell you I'm going golfing, but I'm really going to the nudie bars, you'll know.''

''You go to nudie bars?''

"I said when I'm eighty. You're getting off track here, Julie. And you haven't answered me yet."

Oh God, oh God, oh God. "I can't. Not yet. First I have to say this, Mike. You've been here in Tampa for a year. Before that, Boston. Before that, Atlanta. The FBI moves you a lot. And that's your career. But I have to think about mine. What if you're transferred? What do we do then?"

"That's a tough one, I admit. All I can say is, before I even met you, I talked to my boss about staying in one place, since Aaron is getting close to school age. They guaranteed me three more years here. That's the best I can do. But a lot can happen in three years. I may not want to stay on with the FBI. You may not want to stay at the bank. We could be new parents by then. I know that's not really an answer, but we could be completely different people in three years with whole new priorities. Anything can happen."

"And already has." The time for keeping secrets was over. This was what Rosie meant about her waiting, about talking with Mike first. The stinker knew, which meant Sal knew, that Mike was going to propose to her tonight. So, therefore, did her mother, she'd just bet. And her father. Which explained the party. This was a stinking conspiracy, that's what it was.

"What do you mean, 'and already has'?"

There it was. The question. Julie pushed at his chest, finally sending him back a step. "I'm pregnant, you big jerk."

Mike quit breathing. His mouth dropped. His eyes bulged. His face turned red. Julie observed all these things with clinical detachment while time stood still. *Was he finally going to just explode? Yes.*

"You're pregnant?" he screamed out, loud enough to be heard in Miami. No, Key West. No, Cuba.

Out of the corner of her eye, Julie saw about fifty heads pop around the corner from the living room. Behind her, she heard Aaron stir. "Yes, I am. So it's a good thing you want to marry me, isn't it?"

Mike grinned. "You're pregnant? That time in the bathroom, right?"

The explosion of heat in her face was fanned by all the eyebrows being raised behind Mike. Julie took his arm and turned him around. "We have company, dear."

Mike faced them all, still grinning like a fool, and pointed to Julie. "She's pregnant. We're getting married."

No one standing anywhere near her parents said anything. Julie reached over and snapped one of Mike's suspenders. It worked. He looked down at her. "I haven't said yes to anything yet, big guy."

Mike immediately and melodramatically dropped to one knee. Julie stared at him, disbelieving. Before she could say a word, though, the bedroom door behind her opened up and Aaron sleepily stepped out to nonchalantly sit on his father's knee.

As if that weren't awkward enough, her father bellowed out, "Hold on, right there, young man. Aren't you forgetting something?"

Mike clutched at Aaron to steady him and turned to Jack Cochran. "You said I could marry her."

Jack waved that away. "The cakes, man. The cakes."

"The cakes!" Mike jumped up, nearly unsettling Aaron, who gripped his father's neck tightly and squawked in protest.

Everyone but Julie seemed to know about the damned cakes. Because everyone but Julie murmured, "The cakes."

"All right, that does it." All gazes swung back to her. "What are these cakes everyone is talking about?"

With his son draped over his arm, Mike grinned at her. "I made a cake for you. I decorated it myself. Aaron made one, too."

He may as well have just told her they'd fashioned a

nuclear power plant in their apartment all by themselves. "You two made cakes for me?"

"Yeah. You want to see them?"

She looked from his beloved face, seeing her entire future shining in his eyes, and then turned briefly to the ogling, expectant crowd at the other end of the hallway. They grinned as one. But her mother stood out, tears shining in her eyes. She saw her father put his arm around his wife's shoulders. Behind them stood a beaming Sal Pomerantz, his arm around Rosie's shoulders. She grinned from ear to ear. Julie shook her head at all these sentimental silly people she loved and turned back to Mike. "Tell me the cakes are not in the bathroom."

He hefted and resettled his son's weight on his arm. "The cakes are not in the bathroom."

"Thank God. Okay, let's go see them."

The crowd parted as readily as the Red Sea had for Moses when Mike, Julie and Aaron passed through. Mike, his free hand at her elbow, ushered Julie into the dining room. The revelers flowed around them.

There on the table, as centerpieces, were two, off-center, godawful purple cakes, one rectangular, one round. With tears in her eyes, Julie stared down at the loving creations. She turned into Mike's arm. "Oh, Mike, they are so beautiful," she said into his shirt.

Aaron, still in his father's arms but fully awake now, tried to turn her face back to the table. "Read them, Julie, read them. I told Daddy what to write on mine. Read them to neverbody, okay?"

Julie smiled up into Mike's eyes. "I love you," she mouthed. He winked, his black eyes suspiciously shiny. Julie turned to the cakes. "All right, everybody. Aaron's says, 'Julie, will you be my 'nother mommy?'"

Julie took her finger and wrote "yes" in the frosting and poked it into Aaron's bird-mouth. "You bet I will, big guy."

Her family and friends all sighed. Several people patted

her, Mike, Aaron and her hand-holding parents. Julie smiled and wiped her finger off with a napkin before kissing Aaron's soft cheek. He leaned out of his father's arms to grab her and pop a huge, smacking kiss on her cheek. "I love you, Julie."

"I love you, too, sweetie."

"Aw, now you're gettin' all mushy. Come on, read the other one, already," Sal entreated. "We're starvin' for cake here."

Mike laughed at his partner. "You just want to be my best man."

"Nope, can't do it for you, buddy. Julie here asked me to be her maid of honor if she ever got married. And I accepted."

"You're going to be a maid of honor? I don't know why I hang out with you, Pomerantz."

"Because you love me, Mikey. Admit it."

Mike looked around to see everyone looking at him. And then back at his partner. "Not here, Sal."

Amid catcalls and hooting, attention shifted back to Julie. She raised an edge of the rectangular cake so everyone could see it, and then, her voice choking up with love, she said, "It has a big heart on it, and in the middle it says 'Mike Loves Julie.'" She lowered the cake and began to cry.

Someone must have taken Aaron from Mike because she found herself enfolded in his arms. She clutched at him and cried her ever-loving eyes out while he held her. After several moments, Mike held her away from him and smoothed away her tears with his thumbs. He then cupped her face in his hands. "I love you, Julie."

Seeing now that everyone else had wandered back to the living room, tactfully giving the two lovebirds time alone, she grinned up at him. "I know. I read your cake."

"You never have answered me, you know."

"You never have asked me, you know. Aaron's the only one who's asked so far tonight."

"Great. It's not enough that I bake for you. Now you're going to stand on ceremony. The next thing you'll want is a ring better than the one Sal gave you. Women. You're never satisfied." With a heavy dramatic sigh, Mike reached into his green shirt pocket and produced a real gold ring with a large diamond solitaire on it. Pretending to be piqued, he pulled Sal's ring off her greenish finger, stuck it in his pocket, and then slid his ring in its place. "Okay, will you marry me, so our baby and Aaron can experience the joys of sibling rivalry?"

Julie eyed the ring with openmouthed disbelief and then laughed into his strong, handsome face, loving every line, every plane, every contour. "Yes, Mike, I'll marry you."

"Thank God," he pronounced, slumping slightly. "Celibacy is killing me. Did you know I had to promise your father two weeks ago not to touch you until your last name is DeAngelo?"

Julie laughed out loud in shock and embarrassment. "You're kidding? No wonder you rushed this, you horny devil."

"And you're surprised? I've had all I can take of a monk's life. Listen, your mom wants you to have a huge wedding, all the trimmings, all the relatives here, things like that. I want all that, too, but I'll never make it. I'll explode, certain parts going first. I've got to have some relief."

"We won't have to wait long, Mike. Remember, I'm pregnant. Mom'll put a wedding together in no time, you'll see." Something he'd just said struck her anew. She pulled back from him. "By the way, how often do you talk to my mother?"

Mike resorted to grumpiness. "Every now and then. I like her. After all, she introduced me to the woman I love."

Julie pinched his rock-hard arm. "You are such a big softie."

Mike tugged her firmly against him. "Uh-uh. Feel again."

Julie squealed in, well, maidenly shock. "Mike De-Angelo. You're terrible."

"That's not what you said in the bathroom a couple of weeks ago."

The same thought occurred to them at the same time. Together, they breathed, "The bathroom…"

Julie broke the silence. "We don't dare."

"Your father'll kill me if he finds out."

"Yes, he will."

"We can't do this."

Ida walked through the dining room on her way into the kitchen. "Oh, go on. You're getting married. It's the same thing."

"Mother!" Julie broke away from Mike abruptly. "Were you eavesdropping?"

"Of course not. I'm getting a knife to cut Aaron's cake. You two never even noticed it was gone."

They looked at the table. Aaron's cake was gone. They looked at Ida. She put her hands on her hips. "So, are you going or not?"

"Mother!" She looked up at Mike. He was willing. And so was she. But still… She looked back at her mother. "Not with you knowing. I don't think I can—"

"Oh, go on. Be with your man. Like I didn't get pregnant with you in a bathroom—at your Nana's. On Christmas Day. With the entire family sitting in the next room."

Mike burst out laughing. Julie's jaw dropped. "Mother!"

celebrates forty fabulous years!

Crack open the champagne and join us in celebrating Harlequin Romance's very special birthday.

Forty years of bringing you the best in romance fiction—and the best just keeps getting better!

Not only are we promising you three months of terrific books, authors and romance, but a chance to win a special hardbound 40th Anniversary collection featuring three of your favorite Harlequin Romance authors. And 150 lucky readers will receive an **autographed** collector's edition. Truly a one-of-a-kind keepsake.

Look in the back pages of any Harlequin Romance title, from April to June for more details.

Come join the party!

Take 4 bestselling love stories FREE

Plus get a FREE surprise gift!

Special Limited-time Offer

Mail to Harlequin Reader Service®

3010 Walden Avenue
P.O. Box 1867
Buffalo, N.Y. 14240-1867

YES! Please send me 4 free Harlequin Love and Laughter™ novels and my free surprise gift. Then send me 4 brand-new novels every other month, which I will receive months before they appear in bookstores. Bill me at the low price of $2.90 each plus 25¢ delivery per book and applicable sales tax if any*. That's the complete price and a savings of over 10% off the cover prices—quite a bargain! I understand that accepting the books and gift places me under no obligation ever to buy any books. I can always return a shipment and cancel at any time. Even if I never buy another book from Harlequin, the 4 free books and the surprise gift are mine to keep forever.

102 BPA A7EF

Name	(PLEASE PRINT)	
Address	Apt. No.	
City	State	Zip

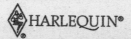

And the Winner Is...
You!

...when you pick up these great titles
from our new promotion at your
favorite retail outlet this June!

Diana Palmer
The Case of the Mesmerizing Boss

Betty Neels
The Convenient Wife

Annette Broadrick
Irresistible

Emma Darcy
A Wedding to Remember

Rachel Lee
Lost Warriors

Marie Ferrarella
Father Goose

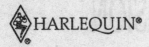 

HE SAID

♥

SHE SAID

Explore the mystery of male/female communication in this extraordinary new book from two of your favorite Harlequin authors.

Jasmine Cresswell and Margaret St. George bring you the exciting story of two romantic adversaries—each from their own point of view!

DEV'S STORY. CATHY'S STORY.
As he sees it. As she sees it.
Both sides of the story!

The heat is definitely on, and these two can't stay out of the kitchen!

Don't miss **HE SAID, SHE SAID.**
Available in July wherever Harlequin books are sold.

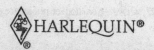

Free Gift Offer

With a Free Gift proof-of-purchase
from any Harlequin® book, you can receive
a beautiful cubic zirconia pendant.

This stunning marquise-shaped stone is a genuine cubic
zirconia—accented by an 18" gold tone necklace.
(Approximate retail value $19.95)

Send for yours today...
compliments of ✥HARLEQUIN®

To receive your free gift, a cubic zirconia pendant, send us one original proof-of-purchase, photocopies not accepted, from the back of any Harlequin Romance®, Harlequin Presents®, Harlequin Temptation®, Harlequin Superromance®, Harlequin Intrigue®, Harlequin American Romance®, or Harlequin Historicals® title available at your favorite retail outlet, together with the Free Gift Certificate, plus a check or money order for $1.65 U.S./$2.15 CAN. (do not send cash) to cover postage and handling, payable to Harlequin Free Gift Offer. We will send you the specified gift. Allow 6 to 8 weeks for delivery. Offer good until December 31, 1997, or while quantities last. Offer valid in the U.S. and Canada only.

Free Gift Certificate

Name: _____

Address: _____

City: _____ State/Province: _____ Zip/Postal Code: _____

Mail this certificate, one proof-of-purchase and a check or money order for postage and handling to: HARLEQUIN FREE GIFT OFFER 1997. In the U.S.: 3010 Walden Avenue, P.O. Box 9071, Buffalo NY 14269-9057. In Canada: P.O. Box 604, Fort Erie, Ontario L2Z 5X3.

FREE GIFT OFFER   084-KEZ

ONE PROOF-OF-PURCHASE
To collect your fabulous FREE GIFT, a cubic zirconia pendant, you must include this original proof-of-purchase for each gift with the properly completed Free Gift Certificate.

084-KEZR